ENTREPRENEUR
5 P.M.
— TO —
9 A.M.

ENTREPRENEUR
5 P.M.
— TO —
9 A.M.

LAUNCHING A PROFITABLE START-UP

WITHOUT QUITTING YOUR JOB

KANTH MIRIYALA
REETHIKA SUNDER

RUPA

Published by
Rupa Publications India Pvt. Ltd 2013
7/16, Ansari Road, Daryaganj
New Delhi 110002

Sales centres:
Allahabad Bengaluru Chennai
Hyderabad Jaipur Kathmandu
Kolkata Mumbai

ISBN: 978-81-291-2393-0

Third impression 2013

10 9 8 7 6 5 4 3

The moral right of the authors has been asserted.

This edition is for sale in the Indian subcontinent only.

Typeset by Jojy Philip, New Delhi.

Printed at Parksons Graphics Pvt. Ltd, Mumbai.

I dedicate this book to my parents, Sunanda and Murthy, my wife, Shaku, my kids, Avani and Akash, my sister, Lakshmi, and to the many mentors and entrepreneurs, past, current and future, that I have had the good fortune of being associated with.

—**Kanth Miriyala**

I dedicate this book to my parents, Shashikala and M. R. Sunder, my mentor and guide, Kanth Miriyala, and to everyone who has touched my life in some way or the other and made it so special.

—**Reethika Sunder**

Contents

Preface
Welcome to the Journey!

This is a guidebook for the first-time entrepreneur. It's also useful for next-time entrepreneurs, in case you have started a business before and want to do better with the next one. And if you are wondering whether you have what it takes, I can address that right away.

A big part of 'what it takes' is simply the desire to create a successful business of your own. That desire is your ticket to the whole entrepreneur's journey. As long as you have it, there is no limit to how far you can go. Just remember it's a journey that will take you away from normal, everyday life. Most people, including a lot of very bright people, never seriously think of being an entrepreneur. They are happy to find a place within some system where they can exercise their talents and earn a living.

Entrepreneur 5 p.m. to 9 a.m. tells you how you can become an entrepreneur even if you have a full-time job and are risk-averse. You can test different business ideas till you find the one that has good potential, start developing it and when it becomes big enough, you can quit your job and work on the start-up full-time. A job pays you for what the role/designation does rather than for what you can do, which is why the compensation it pays doesn't justify your capabilities. Owning a business sets you free to use the full potential of all your abilities and interests. Having said that, the kind of examples used in this book are not

all based on part-time entrepreneurship, but I strongly believe these concepts can be used by a part-time entrepreneur. My own journey as an entrepreneur started part-time and the concepts that have been talked about here are what I have learnt by being a part-time entrepreneur before I finally had the financial freedom to quit my job.

We entrepreneurs seem to have a different DNA. Filling a niche in the status quo is not for us; we would rather seek our fortune by carving out a new niche. We are the kind of people who believe, like Steve Jobs, that 'We are here to put a dent in the universe. Otherwise why else even be here?'

But of course a trip of this sort requires more than desire. You have to choose a suitable destination—a good business to start with—and figure out the best way to get there. You'll want to learn how to travel light and travel smart, so you don't break down or run out of gas at a dead end.

Which is where this book comes in handy. It's a streamlined version, as simple as I can make it, of all the things I wish somebody had sat down and taught me when I first became an entrepreneur, years ago. I made a lot of mistakes and had multiple failures. Surely you can learn from them!

I've also had a few successes and you can learn from them as well. Along with lessons from my own experience, I've shared stories about start-ups I have witnessed, and insights I have gained from other authors. I will urge you to read their books too, after starting with this one, for an all-around guide that may help you reduce your risks and raise your chances of success.

Some of the advice you find here will seem paradoxical. This book encourages you to fail and fail often—but keep the cost of each failure low, so that you can keep going until you succeed. That is the fundamental nature of success: it's hidden among failures.

In my career as a founder, investor and mentor to start-ups, some notable failures were companies that:

- Tried to provide services for patenting out of India, about a decade ago.
- Built resorts in forests! (After building a couple, the management team lost their 'enthusiasm' and we investors barely got our original investment back.)
- Tried online marketing of various kinds of goods and services until the founders exhausted their savings and had to go back to their jobs.

My successes include:

- Mercadence, a software services firm that was profitable and remained profitable in spite of the Internet melt-down in 2000-2001.
- Quintant, a BPO (business process outsourcing) company based in Bangalore, India, which I co-founded with a few friends; sold to iGATE in 2003.
- Qik, a mobile video streaming company in which I was an angel investor, sold to Skype in January 2011.

And I am currently involved in a few start-ups whose (success) stories I hope to tell you in the future.

Right now, though, this is about *your* future. Your entrepreneurial journey is *needed*. The world needs it.

Entrepreneurs are people who pursue their dreams and in the process, build businesses that provide jobs and useful goods for many other people. If this book can help you create a start-up that not only fulfils your wishes but makes a difference in the world—which you just might do—it will be a successful journey for everyone.

—**Kanth Miriyala**

1

Zero to Launch
The Roadmap

The steps and principles you are about to learn can be applied to start-ups in many different fields. Together, these steps and principles make up a 'roadmap' for finding the optimum path from point A to point B—from the very beginning of the start-up process to a *sustainable* launch.

And since we are going from point A to point B, let's start by taking on the simplest and most basic question imaginable. What, exactly, is point A?

Some people may tell you that every new business begins with an idea, but I beg to differ. It begins with a decision. The start-up journey, like every journey, begins with the decision to begin.

Once you have decided, for whatever reasons, that you want to start your own business, you are at point A—a stage that is potentially life-changing. (I say 'potentially' because a big challenge, for many of us, is just to go further than point A. Time and again in these pages we'll see how to move beyond the things that can stop us!)

At point A you might have a specific idea for a product and a company, or no idea at all, just yet. It really does not matter. The biggest asset you begin with is yourself. This includes:

- Your *strengths*—what you are good at.
- Your *passions*—what you love doing.
- Your *money-making abilities*—what you can do that will produce income.
- Your *purposes*—what you dream of accomplishing in life.

Getting clear on who you are, while looking at the needs and options that exist in the marketplace, will help you develop an idea for a business that you are likely to enjoy building. It will also get your business off to a better-than-average start along the road to success.

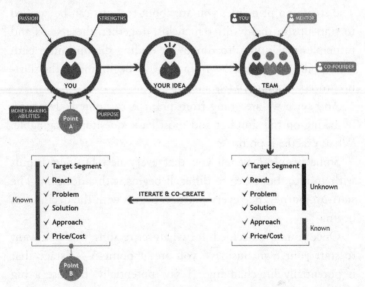

Next, unless you want to have a one-person business, you will need to put together a team. A typical start-up team consists of you, your mentor and usually one or two co-founders.

By the time your team is assembled, you've done a good bit of work on your start-up, and that work will now ramp up in earnest. But you are still not at point B, the point of 'launch'.

Not even if you have incorporated and put up a website. Not even if you're already interacting with customers (as you should be, by now) and making some early sales.

You will truly reach point B, launch, when your business is primed to lift off like a rocket from a launching pad—capable of building and sustaining momentum, clearly aimed and targeted with 'all systems go'.

The way to get there is by a process of iteration. You will test and re-test various aspects of the business, until the major unknowns (things you're uncertain of, or have no clue about) are converted to knowns. The key parameters you need to know clearly are as follows. Some of these may be known and others unknown to you when you begin:

- Target segment—Who would be interested in buying your product or service?
- Reach—How do you reach the people in your target segment?
- Problem—What is their problem or need that you're going to address?
- Solution—What is your solution to the problem?
- Approach—How do you convert your target segment into paying customers?
- Price/Cost—What is your customer willing to pay and how much does it cost for you to deliver the solution?

When all parameters are known, and you have working systems to deliver the solution to people who will pay you more than your cost, you're on your way!

There is a long ride to come after point B, with many more course corrections and adjustments. But, by using a sound roadmap to point B, you will be *ready*.

Let's see how one person travelled from point A to point B.

2

The SP Story

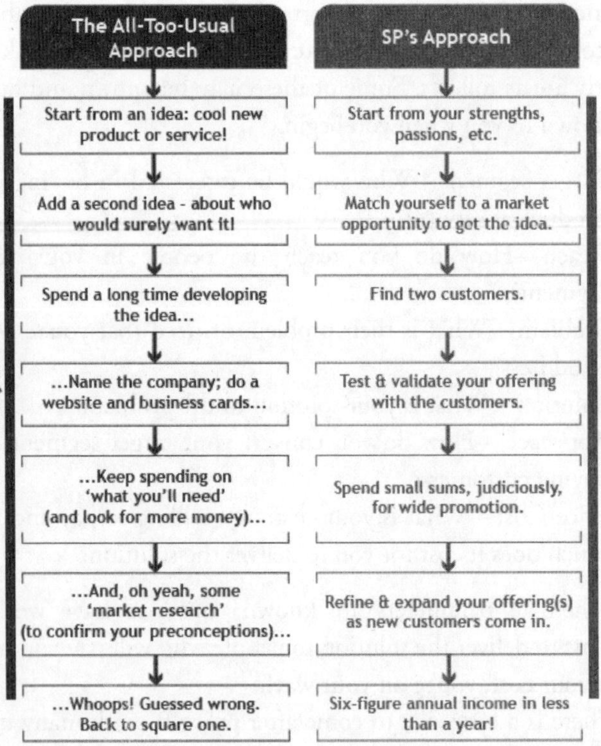

The All-Too-Usual Approach
SP's Approach
Start from an idea: cool new product or service!
Start from your strengths, passions, etc.
Add a second idea - about who would surely want it!
Match yourself to a market opportunity to get the idea.
Spend a long time developing the idea...
Find two customers.
...Name the company; do a website and business cards...
Test & validate your offering with the customers.
...Keep spending on 'what you'll need' (and look for more money)...
Spend small sums, judiciously, for wide promotion.
...And, oh yeah, some 'market research' (to confirm your preconceptions)...
Refine & expand your offering(s) as new customers come in.
...Whoops! Guessed wrong. Back to square one.
Six-figure annual income in less than a year!
1 or 2 years
Less than 1 year

'Entrepreneurship is "risky" mainly because so few of the so-called entrepreneurs know what they are doing,' wrote Peter

Drucker, the famous business guru, back in the 1980s while trying to urge a smarter approach. Unfortunately his words remain all too true today.

Among the people who move beyond point A, a common mistake is going too far down the wrong road right out of the gate. They are so excited that they don't do proper reality testing until they've burned a lot of time and money, or just crashed and burned.

A friend of mine, Swadeep Pillarisetti (let's call him SP from hereon) luckily did not take that route. He couldn't afford it. SP was forced by circumstances to generate cash pretty quickly. He had lost his job and had taken another that paid only half of his family's living expenses. Then, to make matters worse, he was fired from that one. That was the straw that broke the camel's back...the 'camel,' in this case, being his long-held belief that he had to plod through life working for other people.

SP decided to venture out on his own. He had joined a network marketing business to make some money on the side, but hadn't given it much attention because until he was fired, he had been working full-time. Network marketing business is a method of direct selling of products in which the sales force is compensated not only for the sales they personally generate but also for the sales of the other salespeople they recruit. This recruited sales force is referred to as the participant's down line.

Building up that side business to the point where he was in charge and earning a serious income would take far too long. Thus began a rather urgent search for alternatives.

To begin with, SP did possess some qualities that were barely utilized in the job he had just lost. He had a degree from a fine university and was really good at math. Also, he loved teaching.

And SP had been wise enough to find mentors, people in his life to whom he could turn for advice. One of his mentors

suggested he go to a website that would connect him to parents of students who needed a math tutor. Within days, he was teaching two students and generating real cash.

The website operators were keeping a sizable portion of his pay as their cut, but that was okay. Something wonderful had just happened. He had validated a market segment, finding that there were students in his city whose parents were willing to pay a significant hourly rate for math tutoring. He had also confirmed that he loved teaching math. And better yet, the students liked him and his teaching methods.

SP then had an *Aha!* moment: *Maybe I can find the students myself and keep all the money, instead of paying the middlemen.* As for how to reach those students and their parents, why not try multiple ways? Using some of his new income he mounted a broad advertising campaign: word-of-mouth, newspaper ads, Craigslist, videos and the Internet. He started getting more and more students directly.

As he taught, SP also got direct feedback on who needed help with what. He kept refining his offerings, developing specific one-on-one 'classes' in topics such as ACT Math and calculus. He was acquiring a much more 'targeted' sense of his target segments and learning how he could price his tutoring as well.

In less than one year he broke through to a six-figure annual income—doing work that he enjoyed, with prospects for further growth ahead!

Let's recap how SP followed the Zero to Launch roadmap. Early on, he identified his own assets. His:

- Strength was math;
- Passion was teaching;
- Money-making ability (in this case, a simple convergence of the above two) was teaching math; and

- Purpose was to urgently make enough money to support his family.

Some people with the same Strength, Passion and Money-making ability might go back to college to get a teaching certificate, then look for a job in a school as a math teacher. But Sam's Purpose ruled out that slower and costlier path, and besides, he had decided to seek a more entrepreneurial path. All of this led to a (fairly obvious) idea—tutoring—in which he got a foothold as an independent contractor and then took charge to build his own business.

Within that line of business, he had been able to rapidly confirm three of the key parameters as 'knowns'. Clearly there was a Target Segment with a Problem for which he had a Solution. When he set out on his own, the other three parameters of Reach, Approach and Price/Cost were all 'unknown' to varying degrees. He wasn't sure how to reach new prospects. He had a better sense, but still wasn't sure how to convert the prospects to steady customers and how much he could charge.

So he used a process of iteration. Through ongoing testing and re-testing, he converted the unknowns to knowns and refined *all* the parameters as well. By then, he was at lift-off.

You may say: Wait a minute. What about team-building? Well, as we noted, SP had mentors in place. And during that first year he didn't need co-founders.

One big reason to bring co-founders on board is to complement your strengths, thereby filling out the skill set your start-up needs. For instance, in a high-tech start-up, maybe you have the 'front-end' people skills required to build a customer base, but you need a co-founder with the back-end skills to make the technology work well. SP discovered he had all the skills to run a tutoring business, so he stayed solo.

Will SP go on being a one-person shop? As I write this, he hasn't yet decided, but his options are open.

He has definitely put himself in a position to add employees and partners, and grow a full-fledged tutoring company if he wishes. He is truly at point B because his operations are *scalable*. He now has *systems* in place that are expandable and repeatable.

His advertising system reaches his target segments effectively, and it could either be expanded in his home city or replicated in other cities. Although his students like him personally, what they really benefit from are the teaching methods and systems that he has worked out, right down to specific 'classes' for specific math needs. Other good people are out there, whom he could hire to teach for him, using his methods. He could even copyright the classes he's developed.

And if SP should need investors for growth, he can show them a nice package. He won't just be asking them to make a bet on a smart guy with an idea. He can offer them a chance to buy into working systems that have been proven to produce cash flow.

Point B is where someone has found a business they like, they have found a target segment that is willing to use it and willing to pay for it. The product-market fit has been found. The business may or may not have become profitable by this time. Google and Facebook are examples of organizations that figured out how to become profitable much later. He can tell them that lift-off is in progress and now is the time to hop aboard, and he'll be telling the truth. That's the power of point B!

3

A Disclaimer

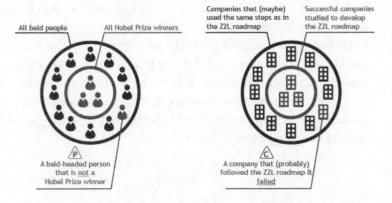

Now it's time to give you a consumer warning. For that, I will use my dad's favourite example. Let us imagine for a minute that all Nobel Prize winners are bald. This is obviously not true in reality, but imagine it is. My dad makes an important point that I would like you to understand.

In the Disclaimer graphic, at the top, the big circle contains ALL of the world's bald-headed people. The smaller circle within it contains ALL Nobel Prize winners. Clearly, every single Prize winner is bald-headed, but does that mean that everyone who goes bald wins a Nobel Prize? Not necessarily. Person P is one of many who doesn't have a Nobel Prize to his name. Thus, going bald will get you in the hunt but there are no guarantees.

Likewise, the Z2L roadmap was created by looking at what successful start-ups have done based on personal involvement and experience with them and by reading books by eminent authors on this subject. I can say that if you use the roadmap, it will put you firmly in the hunt and raise your chances of success—probably far more than the odds of winning a Nobel—but even with the wisest of approaches, many entrepreneurs fail.

Sometimes you take your best shot and you just miss, because the world of start-ups can be tricky: You are building your gun while aiming it and the targets are moving. The question then is, what will you do next? My advice is: Try again!

Suppose your goal is to get hit by an airplane. This book is putting you on a runway and showing you how to run towards landing planes, so that sooner or later you are likely to collide with one. No guarantees! However, as SP, the math teacher, would say, increasing the number of attempts will increase your chances of scoring a hit.

4
You!

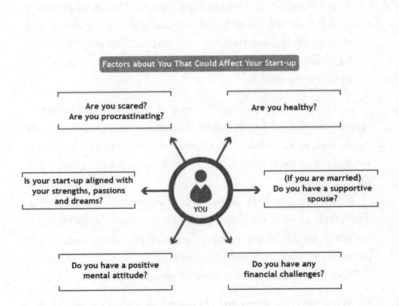

Factors about You That Could Affect Your Start-up

Are you scared?
Are you procrastinating?

Are you healthy?

Is your start-up aligned with
your strengths, passions
and dreams?

YOU

(If you are married)
Do you have a supportive
spouse?

Do you have a positive
mental attitude?

Do you have any
financial challenges?

Let's return now to point A, your decision to start a business. From this point, we'll use the rest of the book to go through the roadmap in greater depth, at a level where you can actually apply the steps and principles to your start-up.

The very first step is about YOU. Where do you stand in your life right now? And what kind of person are you? Each question can be broken out into several factors. Let's start with where you stand in life:

- How healthy are you? A start-up takes a lot of time and energy, and good health will enable you to pursue the work better.
- How is your relationship with your spouse or partner, if you have one? An unhappy, unstable or 'high-maintenance' relationship could drain you and distract you.
- Do you have pressing financial problems? Although the need for money can be a motivator, severe financial pressures could make it hard to focus on your start-up, or they could skew your decision making—for instance, driving you to do whatever will bring in cash in a hurry, rather than what's right for the start-up.

If you are facing challenges in one or more areas, that doesn't mean you should forget about launching a start-up. It does mean you need to take the challenges into account. Can you work around these issues? What could you do to improve your life situation?

The key fact is: *Your start-up will affect your life and vice versa.* Therefore, as we'll see shortly, it's best to take a 'well-rounded' approach to the whole process—even if you don't have major problems in your personal life at present.

Now let's re-examine the kind of person you are.

- What are your strengths? Have you identified them?
- What are your passions? (These are the activities you delight in, the ones that literally make you 'light up' with energy.)
- What are your dreams, desires and goals? Put another way: What are your purposes in life? How clearly do you know them?

By taking inventory of yourself in this simple way, you can set out to *conceive and organize* a start-up that will draw on your strengths, engage your passions and align with your purposes in life. That's the route to a better business and a happier you. But

before we get into the details of taking such an inventory, here is one more question:

- How positive is your mental attitude? How confident and optimistic are you?

This will determine your ability to convince others of the value of your start-up: co-founders, investors, prospective employees and clients. Your attitude will also determine whether you can overcome the obstacles you meet along the way—including the obstacles that keep many people from ever getting started!

In the next few pages we'll look at three common obstacles and some ways of adjusting your attitude to conquer them.

5

The Fear Factor

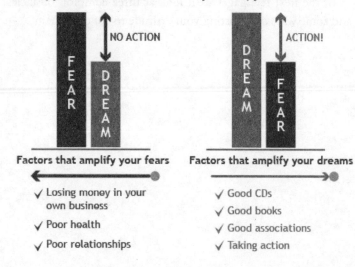

When fear is greater than your dream, you don't take action

NO ACTION

FEAR

DREAM

Factors that amplify your fears

←————————●

✓ Losing money in your own business
✓ Poor health
✓ Poor relationships

When your dream is greater than your fear, you take action

ACTION!

DREAM

FEAR

Factors that amplify your dreams

————————→●

✓ Good CDs
✓ Good books
✓ Good associations
✓ Taking action

Franklin D. Roosevelt once said, 'The only thing we have to fear is fear itself.' While there may be other legitimate threats in life, 'fear itself' is the factor that prevents more people from launching a start-up than any other.

The Fear Factor graph shows how this happens. If the fear you feel is greater than the strength of your dreams and desires, then fear prevails, and as Roosevelt noted, it 'paralyses needed

efforts' to move forward. You procrastinate endlessly, frozen in a state of inaction. How many friends do you know who've been telling you they need to start their own business, but haven't?

You need to reduce the fear while feeding the dreams and desires, to swing the balance to a positive differential. And there are practical steps for doing this. For instance, a big part of fear is uncertainty. Right away, you may run into problems you don't know how to solve—or you worry you won't be able to solve them—so you stop. The fear of the unknown is paralysing you. But what if you tried learning something that converts the unknown to a known?

Here's an example: You have an idea for a cloud-based email backup service. It backs up email so your Outlook has very few messages and runs fast all the time. The trouble is, you don't know how to test the idea with 100 prospective users, and you procrastinate. Then you attend a marketing webinar. You get a step-by-step approach on how to use LinkedIn and Facebook to test your Business-to-Consumer (B2C) start-up idea.

Now you are very excited. Just by gaining some knowledge, you've reduced the fear factor…and now that you know what to do next, your dreams and desires are fired up too. That propels you into action. These are some things that can feed your fears:

- Uncertainty about how to proceed; not knowing how-to or what-to.
- Having failed in business before, perhaps losing a lot of your own money along with friends' and family's money.
- Poor health, a poor relationship or poor finances.
- Hanging around people who are negative about entrepreneurship or have an employee mentality.

Conversely, these are some ways to reduce your fears and/or feed your dreams and desires:

- Reading books or listening to business CDs whenever time permits, to build your knowledge base.
- Attending seminars or webinars by people who have successfully built their own businesses.
- Hanging around entrepreneurs.
- Losing a job could increase your motivation dramatically, as it did for SP (though I don't wish this upon you).

But above all, here is a step that always works:

- *Taking action*, for action cures fear quite rapidly.

What kind of action? *Any* action that moves you in a positive direction towards launching your start-up. Identify something that will help, then do it, then do the next thing.

This is the most direct approach. You are changing your attitude by changing your behaviour. You are turning the inertia of fear into the momentum of action—and transforming yourself from a fear person to an action person.

Of course, instead of taking action, you can wait until circumstances drive you to action…if they ever do.

Until SP lost his second job, his inertia was very high. His first job loss hadn't motivated him enough to get serious about starting a business. Although the second job was not paying all his bills, he still had some money coming in.

Many of us have heard the story of Johnny and his moaning dog. When a friend asked why the dog was moaning, Johnny said, 'Because he is sitting on a nail!'

'Then why doesn't he get up?'

'Because it does not hurt bad enough!'

This summarizes the plight of many people who are in jobs they don't like, and yet refrain from taking action. Many never will.

When SP lost his second job he was forced into entrepreneurship. To his credit, he went after it aggressively and made it happen in short order. However, he was also fortunate to find a business that could pay off as quickly and generously as it did.

It's better by far to begin the start-up process *while you are employed.* That gives you a steady source of income, plus the chance to make contacts or gain experience that could help you.

But here is where many employed people perceive another obstacle to building a start-up. They'll say, 'I don't have the time!'

6

A Fuzzy Calendar

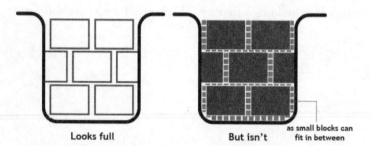

| Looks full | But isn't | as small blocks can fit in between |

Prospective entrepreneurs say 'I don't have time to start a business' for one of two reasons: Either they are scared (and time is just an excuse), or they have a fuzzy calendar.

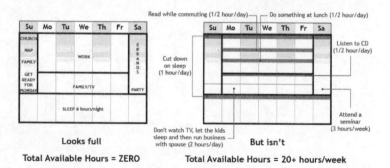

Looks full

Total Available Hours = ZERO

But isn't

Total Available Hours = 20+ hours/week

A typical work week for Kanth before he began to explore entrepreneurship used to be to leave for office at 6 a.m., take

the train at 6.30 a.m., be in office at 7.15 a.m., have breakfast, read the newspaper and start work at around 8 a.m. The lunch break would be about an hour. He would get home by 7.30 p.m. every day, have dinner, talk to his wife and kids and sleep at around 10 p.m. The weekends would generally include running errands, socializing, partying, taking rest and preparing for the work grind on Monday.

When Kanth started venturing out and exploring entrepreneurship, he tried to look at his schedule and see how he could find time for doing something new. And when he critically examined his schedule, he realized that he easily had around 15 hours on weekdays and another 20 hours on weekends. He could use this time for developing the concept, market testing with potential users, preparing a mock up, entering business expenses and other such tasks. So Kanth discovered that all this time he had a fuzzy calendar.

A fuzzy calendar is one that looks filled up when it isn't. It's the kind that many people carry in their minds, so they are unable to 'see' any 'free time'. What they really mean is this: 'All my time is taken by some activity or other right now. I don't have any time when I am sitting around doing nothing.' Prioritizing and better use of small chunks of time can usually solve this problem.

Imagine you have a container and some blocks of differing sizes. The big blocks represent important things in your day. They go in first. After that the container appears full, but you can put in many smaller blocks in the spaces in between. Then you might be able to squeeze in still smaller blocks. Finally, you might be able to pour in water to fill the remaining space!

The big blocks in your day might be your job and your family time. But then you can squeeze in many small blocks:

- How do you commute to work and how do you use that time? If you drive, you can listen to CDs and learn. If you

ride a commuter train, your options increase: You can read, work at your laptop or do business over the phone.

- You can't work on your start-up while you are on the job, but what about at lunchtime? You could leave the building and find a place where you're able to do all sorts of things while eating, from phone meetings to web research.

- Next, look at your evenings at home. Maybe after the children are in bed, you can put a couple of hours into your start-up. Maybe your spouse or partner will help you with it!

- Finally, some of the things we do to 'relax' aren't really so relaxing, and we don't need to spend as much time on them as we do. Try cutting down on party time, or TV time (by disconnecting the cable TV) or time wasted on the Internet.

These items add up to three to four hours per day; that's over 20 hours a week. You can make plenty of progress with your start-up in that time. And if you have a co-founder doing the same, your progress is even greater.

7
No Money

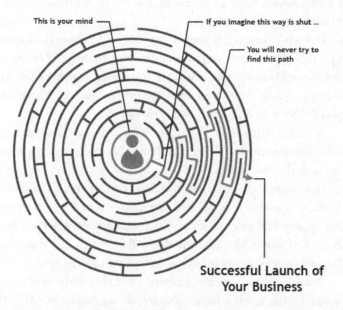

This is your mind

If you imagine this way is shut ...

You will never try to find this path

Successful Launch of Your Business

Another common objection I hear is, 'I have no money.' What the person usually means is: 'Okay, maybe I'm not deeply in debt or living from hand to mouth, but I don't have any extra cash either.' Or something like: 'Doing a start-up could eat up the savings I've put away as a contingency fund.'

What we have here is nothing but a wrong affirmation that has, over time, created a wrong mental program. In the person's

mind, no money *equals* no start-up, because the person has mentally connected the two so strongly (and wrongly) that they bring his thinking to a halt.

The maze in the illustration shows how this wrong programme works. Your mind is at the centre of the maze. In fact, there is a financial path that would take you to all the way to launching a start-up. However it's a twisting path, not obvious at first. You are going to have to feel your way along, finding smart ways to access and leverage the money that's available to you.

But when you say, 'I have no money, so I cannot do a start-up,' this immediately shuts a door in your mind. *And the mind believes what it tells itself.* Because you closed that door (which doesn't actually exist), you don't even try to open it. Therefore, you NEVER find the path that does exist!

A better affirmation might be: '*Can I* do my own start-up with the money I have?' Or even better, '*I can* do my own start-up with the money I have!'

In my own case, no one in my family had ever built a business. In fact, one of my uncles had ventured out and lost not only his money but also the money of the family members he had borrowed from! So all of the doors that led to my starting a business were—in my mind—shut and shut pretty firmly.

But my dreams were big. I earned a PhD in computer science. Then I took a job which, contrary to my hopes, wasn't very enjoyable and wasn't helping me achieve my dreams. So I started hanging around entrepreneurs. I read Robert Kiyosaki's books *Rich Dad, Poor Dad* and *The Business School.* Slowly my mind started opening up. I found a way out through the maze. And, over time, I began finding success as an entrepreneur.

I had escaped from a mental captivity of my own making. Then I knew that the doors which had been holding me back

were not real. Since my mind had constructed them and locked them, my mind also held the keys that could open them wide.

Here is an example of entrepreneurship on a shoestring.

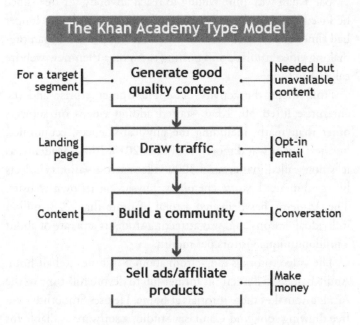

The Khan Academy Type Model

For a target segment — **Generate good quality content** — Needed but unavailable content

Landing page — **Draw traffic** — Opt-in email

Content — **Build a community** — Conversation

Sell ads/affiliate products — Make money

Although it might be considered 'social entrepreneurship', the story of Khan Academy shows that you don't need a huge amount of money to create a global enterprise. Salman Khan, the founder, got started on his idea in the same sort of way my friend SP did: by tutoring teenagers in math. There were some key differences however and he took the idea in a different direction.

Khan, with degrees from MIT and Harvard, was working full-time when he agreed in 2004 to tutor his young cousin Nadia as a favour. Because Nadia lived in another city, he taught her over the phone and online, using a simple shared-

notepad program to sketch out math problems and solutions. Pretty cool! Before long, Nadia's brothers and other kids were asking for help too.

'Sal' Khan was quite willing to teach anybody for free, since he loved doing it, but with the growing demand he no longer had time for personal sessions with each student. He began pre-making video tutorials and posting them on a then-new website called YouTube.

From there, the activity became a true enterprise and the enterprise lifted off. Khan started adding videos on subjects other than math, including the physical sciences, economics, business, history and more. As of early 2013, Khan Academy, as it is now called, has around 3000 videos across various subjects like arithmetic, history, chemistry, physics on its own website. The Academy has delivered a total of more than 228 million individual 'lessons' and was attracting students at a rate of about a million unique visitors per month.

The video tutorials range from about 5 minutes to half-hour. And Khan, who has left his former job to devote full-time to the Academy, makes these tutorials at home. He uses Smoothdraw, a free drawing tool, and Camtasia Studio, a software available for a couple of hundred dollars! The Academy's vision is to create 'the world's first free, world-class virtual school.'

Entrepreneurship on a Shoestring

Several staff members have joined Salman Khan to help run this literally 'free' enterprise. Khan Academy supports itself entirely through donations; the last donation was of $5 million from the O'Sullivan Foundation—not much, in today's big-budget world, but enough to fund the work.

What can we learn from this? Enterprises are created by passion,

vision and persistence, not always with money. Some enterprises might need money—a lot of money—in order to create and grow. (I am thinking of biotech companies, for example.) But many exciting enterprises can be created without much funding to speak of. In fact, ironically, it appears as though the lack of money can be a blessing in disguise. It's a constraint that forces significant efficiencies into the process, early on, helping a new start-up achieve profitability and growth more rapidly than a well-funded business.

What content can you produce in large amounts that people may want? And what can you sell to the traffic attracted by your content? Can that create affiliate commissions for you? Now there's a simple, low-cost start-up concept!

What Do You Really Want?

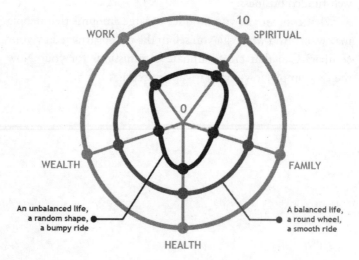

'What do you really want?' is perhaps the most important question in life. While any of us could come up with a variety of answers, there is a simple answer that applies to all of us, including to you. You want happiness.

And the old cliché is true: Money can't buy it.

If you have success in your start-up but you have a vacuum in your heart, spiritually, will you be happy? No. Maybe you love working on your business, but if it becomes so all-consuming that it wrecks your health and your relationships with the people

you love, will you be happy? No. We need balance in life to have a quality life.

You might know the sickening thumpety-thump feeling of driving a car down the highway with a wheel that's 'out of balance'—or how it feels to ride a bicycle on a wheel that's badly 'out of round'. So the illustration invites you to think of yourself on a wheel rolling through this world of ours.

Each spoke of the wheel represents one aspect of life: health, wealth, family, the rewards of work and spiritual well-being. (Your wheel could have other spokes, depending on what you value.) Each spoke is also the axis of a graph, reflecting how well you're doing in that area on a 0-to-10 scale: zero, at the centre, is 'not at all', while 10, at the outermost rim, is the best you could do.

When you connect the dots, what do you get? If you have an 8 in all areas, or better yet a 9 or a 10, then not only are you doing great, you are well-rounded. The vehicle of your life is going to give you a nice smooth ride, running on a set of these perfect-circle wheels. But if you've been pumping up your score in some areas at the expense of others, you are going to go bumping along that road on wheels that are out of kilter—maybe so badly that they throw you off the course you are trying to steer, and you wind up in a ditch. And if you let one or two areas deflate all the way to zero, now you've got a flat. The best you can do is try to limp to the repair shop.

When Kanth looks back at his quality of life before he started his entrepreneurial ventures, he recalls that he was out of home for 14 hours every day during the weekdays. His two-year-old son would refuse to talk to him on the weekends as he was upset with him for being out of home for most part of the week. His finances were not in great shape either, with just some small savings made possible with the job. His health too was suffering

due to the schedule and diet with a cholesterol count of 250 for a 32-year-old. On the spiritual front, however, he had done nothing, not even read the Bhagavad Gita.

When Kanth realized how he could utilize his time better, he was able to develop other sources of income through network marketing. He was able to better manage his health by taking time out for workout and his cholesterol dropped by 80 points. He also spent 15 minutes a day reading the pocket Bhagavad Gita and by end of the year he managed to read it around 20 times! All of this helped bring more balance and happiness to his life.

Entrepreneurs need to remember that 'balance' isn't just a nice thing to have. It's necessary. While making a difference is important, and creating wealth is exciting, none of these things alone is enough to sustain a human being, and your ability to achieve any of them depends on the shape you are in.

As Glenn Bland says in *Success, The Glenn Bland Method*, God probably intended us to have—above everything else—balance in life. In fact, Bland defines success as: 'The progressive realization of predetermined worthwhile goals, stabilized with balance and purified by belief'.

That's one of the best definitions of *success* I have read.

Strengths, Passions and Making Money
The Sweet Spot

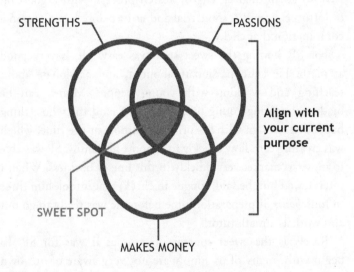

There's an old folk saying, 'The fox has a thousand tricks; the hedgehog only one, but it always works.' The business consultant Jim Collins borrowed from this to create what he calls the Hedgehog Concept: The way to succeed in business is by doing one thing really, really well.

Then how do you find that one thing to focus your business on? The one that will make the business lift off, and enable you to enjoy building and running the business? The answer lies in the 'sweet spot' where your strengths, passions and money-making abilities intersect. It will be something you are very good at—Collins invites you to aim high, asking what you can be 'the best in the world at'—as well as something you love doing and that will produce income.

If those three come together and are also aligned with your purposes in life, then you have found your niche, your big idea. Doesn't that sound easy? For some people it is. Others may have to go through a lengthy search process, with a good bit of introspection plus some trial and error before hitting upon a combination that clicks.

For SP, finding the sweet spot was easy. He is very good at math. He's also passionate about it, and passionate about teaching and working with young people. Money can be made by tutoring young people in math, and the whole thing happened to align with his primary purpose at the time, which was creating cash flow quickly to support his family. SP was able to move to market very quickly in this line of business. When I interviewed him he said, tongue in cheek, that it took him three to four *hours* of preparation time before he was ready to go out and work as a math tutor!

Rarely is the sweet spot as obvious as it was for SP. To begin with, many of us simply are not very aware of our own strengths, passions and money-making abilities. You know how a working life goes: Most of the time you are busy just doing what you're doing, in a job and career that you have landed in by some combination of past decisions, chance events and necessity. You may come to define yourself in these limited terms—'this is what I do; that's me'—without reflecting much

on who you actually are and what you *could* do. In the chapter ahead we'll consider how to open up our awareness of these things.

Furthermore, your inner drives and capabilities may not 'converge' upon a sweet-spot business idea as neatly as Sam's did. It's worth generating several ideas persistently until you find something that fits your strengths and matches with your passions. Then—if it makes money—see if you can align that with your dreams and goals.

Here is the sequence that I went through over the past couple of decades:

1. I was working as a strategic technology researcher, which sounds glamorous, but all the job did for me was make money. It was neither my strength nor passion nor aligned with my goals in life.

2. Then I moved into an organizational role, organizing a technology conference that also was neither my strength nor passion, nor aligned with my goals. And I almost got fired! This was a step backward.

3. I jumped into my own business, a start-up in IT consulting. At least that was one of my strengths, though not the best. The type of work involved was not my passion, but it made money, and finally got me pointed in a direction aligned with my longer-term goals, dreams and desires.

4. Then came Quintant, a start-up in the BPO space (later sold to iGATE). This was aligned with my goals and desires, leveraged my strengths in consulting and innovation, made money and was fun, most of the time.

5. From 2007 onward, I understood the Hedgehog Concept and have stayed in the intersection at the sweet spot. I love teaching, coaching and mentoring entrepreneurs and start-

ups. I am good at developing a vision, coming up with innovative ideas, problem-solving and communication. I love to, and thrive at, taking start-ups from point A to point B as described in our Zero to Launch roadmap.

The catch is that such a role does not always pay or pays erratically. I had put myself on a pretty good financial footing from previous earnings and the sale of Quintant, but not enough to be set for life. So I built a network marketing business which provided a reliable stream of passive income. Network marketing is a marketing strategy in which the sales force is compensated not only for sales they personally generate but also for the sales of the other salespeople that they recruit.

That enabled me to go on doing what I loved, advising and investing in start-ups, and it dramatically increased the range of choices I had. I could work with a start-up even if it couldn't afford to pay me, just because I liked the team and the direction. If it failed before reaching point B, as has happened several times, that was all right. If a company succeeded, reaching point B and going beyond to an exit, I made spikes of income.

My journey to finding and living in the sweet spot while achieving my goals was probably more complex and convoluted than usual, but I hope it illustrates the fact that this journey can sometimes take years and a lot of persistence. And it's well worth it, because frankly: When you get there, you are having a blast every day.

How Do You Find Your Strengths?

Strengths are things you can do well, exceptionally well, regardless of whether or not you like doing them.

As the illustration shows, your most valued strengths will be skills that other people need and do not, themselves, commonly

Things where others are looking for help	E.g. Math Tutoring *Your Strength*	E.g. Curing Cancer *No One's Strength*
Things that others do well	E.g. Paying Bills *Common Skills*	E.g. Estate Planning *Not Your Strength*
	Things that you do well	Things that you go to others for help

have. You know you have a strength in a given area when one of the following happens: People come to you for direct help in this area, or they ask you for advice about it, they're willing to pay you for doing it, or you have won appreciation in the past in this area.

1. *People come to you for help with it.* Before he founded Khan Academy, Salman Khan was working in an unrelated field, the investment business. He did not consciously set out to become the world's best-known creator of online tutorials. He discovered he had a singular strength in this area after tutoring his cousin online, and doing it so well that many other kids were soon coming to him for help.

2. *People ask you for advice about it.* I have a friend; let's call him Danny. Danny is known in our circle as the expert on electronic gadgets, their features and pricing, and the best places to buy them. So we all go to him for advice. SP was 'influenced' by Danny to buy a GPS device from a Thanksgiving sale, standing in the line at 2 a.m. to get one! I had discontinued Vonage service due to poor quality in the past; Danny convinced me to get back on it and use

their unlimited international calling plan, which turned out to be a great bargain for me. Clearly this is one of Danny's strengths but as of now, he does not get paid for it.

3. *People are willing to pay you for it.* Even if you don't have credentials in it or it isn't your primary line of work. Delia (not her real name) is a chemical engineer by background but realized she was really good at drawing illustrations. She started bidding on projects on eLance and, before she knew it, she was earning thousands of dollars working from home.

To find out what *your* strengths are, start paying attention to what other people are telling you.

Try monitoring your incoming phone calls, face-to-face meetings and email inbox for a while, to see what others want from you. If there are recurring patterns in the types of things that people are asking you for, or asking you about—and they aren't part of your normal work duties—then you may be discovering strengths you weren't fully aware of.

Also, monitor yourself. When you have to do something, do you 'do it yourself' or have someone else do it? For example, I go to my wife for help in managing our accounts. And despite being a guy who likes to take charge of his own affairs, I pay other people to do my tax preparation, lawn care and website development. Clearly none of these are strengths of mine. But I do my own planning and goal-setting, not using a consultant; and when a speech has to be made, I write it and deliver it myself. These are strengths. There are people who would like to provide these services for me, but I have learned to do them very well, thank you!

In fact, here is another indication of strength: You look at a piece of work that others have done, and either you step in

to fix it or you say to yourself: 'I can do better than that.' Or you learn that someone has earned money for something and you think: 'I cannot believe he got paid for doing that. Why, anybody could do it—I could do it!' The chances are it is *not* a task that anyone off the street could perform; it may be a particular strength of yours.

When you find that you are 'putting yourself into' a situation in such a manner—either jumping right in to do a certain type of task, or imagining yourself doing it—the chances are that it's more than a strength. It's probably also a passion, something you want to do and would enjoy doing.

How Do You Find Your Passions?

Passions are activities that you love. They are things you do (or would do) without being paid, whether for the sheer joy of doing them or because the subject engages you so deeply. And it's quite possible to have 'hidden passions' you haven't recognized, at least when it comes to thinking about them in relation to a business you might start.

Someone who is close to you might help you identify your passions, but for the most part it's up to you. You can't rely on input from others as much as you do in identifying your strengths. Here you are searching for what makes you light up inside, as distinct from skills you display on the outside. So you'll want to do some introspection.

You could start just by noticing the 'issues' or 'causes' that trigger strong feelings. For example, what makes your blood boil? Does it happen when you see people littering or parents screaming at their kids? When you see people struggling to earn a living? Conversely, what's happening in the world around you that excites you in a positive way?

Observations like this may seem to have little connection with a line of business you could pursue, but take note of them. They give you clues to subjects that arouse your energies—and the clues could lead somewhere you hadn't considered.

Next, pay attention to the things you do proactively. If litter bugs you, maybe you organize a neighbourhood meeting to keep the streets clean. Or, in any clubs or groups that you belong to, perhaps you're the person who always wants to take on a certain type of task. Repeatedly looking to seize the initiative in a given area is a pretty reliable indicator of a passion.

Last but not least, notice the things you put a lot of time and energy into—often without being asked or paid.

Maybe you spend hours on the phone helping a friend with a relationship problem. Or you are visiting your cousin's home for the weekend, and you bring your toolkit so you can spend happy hours fixing everything from the faucets to the children's playset in the back yard. Or, if the President's latest public-policy idea strikes you as wrong, you fire off letters and talk endlessly about why it won't work, backing up your view with data that you have collected and analysed as closely as any pundit on the subject.

Does this mean you ought to start a counselling service, a home-improvement business or a political consulting firm? Not necessarily; the linkage from personal passion to business idea may not be that direct. But you are getting strong indications of the *kind* of activity that turns you on.

You don't even notice time passing when you are doing what engages you deeply. If you can't think of any major activity in your life for which this is true, try watching yourself for a few days to capture the little things that make you feel passionate, if only for brief periods.

It's also possible that you have not yet 'found your passions' because your experiences have been limited. In that case, the prescription is obvious. Go out and have some new experiences! Maybe your passion is waiting to be discovered, in a setting that may have little to do with 'business' or 'work', *as you now conceive it*, and it will lead you where you need to go.

Identifying Your Dreams, Desires and Goals

Whereas your passions are things you love to do, your dreams, desires and goals are things you reach for. Some of these may be specific items you want to accomplish, like 'pay off the mortgage' or 'write a book'. Others are states of being you want to achieve and maintain, like 'be independently wealthy' or 'have a good relationship with mom'.

You've probably heard that it helps to define your goals as clearly as you can, so you can work towards them and know when you are meeting them. Thus, if one of your goals is 'spend more time with my family', you might want to specify blocks of time to set aside. But there is a much more important step that comes before fine-tuning your goals. *Write them down.*

Until you commit your dreams, desires and goals to paper, they are invisible. They may be known only to you, and even you may know them only vaguely. When you put them down, it's the first physical evidence of your goals. You are beginning to create them, manifest them, give them life.

The best way is to sit down, take a piece of paper, and just start writing what you want. Don't think much. Simply list everything you want for yourself or others, from blue-sky dreams to the most practical goals. Write them as they come to mind, in no particular order and without trying to split hairs in the wording.

The next step is to put them in order of importance. For this I use a process described in *The Passion Test* by Janet and Chris Attwood. You could use the process to identify your top passions, but I have also found it useful in prioritizing my goals.

Take the first goal you wrote down (such as 'pay off the mortgage'), compare it with the second ('help my son get into a good college') and see which is more important to you. Then take the 'winner' and compare it with the next goal. Repeat this until you have gone through your goals list. The winner, at the end, is your top-priority goal. Write it down on a separate piece of paper with a '1' next to it, and cross it off the original list.

Now go back to that original list and, starting from the top again, compare all of the runners-up in the same fashion, one pair at a time in a process of elimination. The winner at the end of this round is your second most important goal. Put it on your separate piece of paper with a '2', cross it off the original list, and run the process again. You can keep going until you find your top few goals or until you have ordered them all in a priority list.

Treat this as an ongoing exercise, something you can repeat every few months. Each time your priority list might come out different. That is fine. You change over time and so do your priorities. But eventually you will see them stabilize.

For the purposes of this book, the last step is to separate your prioritized goals into two groups: a group that is likely to be impacted or enabled by your new start-up, such as any financial goal, and a group that isn't ('call mom each week'). The second group still matters to you but those goals will not come into play in considering a start-up.

It may not always be clear at first whether, or how, a particular goal will be impacted. Fo instance spending more time with your family. A start-up that demands long workdays and lots of

travel would probably interfere with that goal, while a business you can run from your home on a flexible schedule could help you achieve it, and others might have no effect one way or the other.

In such a case, keep the goal 'in play' even though the impact is uncertain. If the goal is high on your priority list, it can help you determine the *kind* of business you want to start and the nature of your role in it.

Putting It All Together

Once you have explored your strengths and passions, and clarified your goals, how do you then use this information to identify a business idea that is in your 'sweet spot', where all of the factors come together?

I could try to give instructions for making more lists or charts, but it's really not a systematic, scientific process. It's more of a fluid and intuitive process. Use your feelings as a compass to guide you to the right path. Trust that your enhanced knowledge of yourself will bring forth a business idea.

Don't set a deadline for coming up with a great idea, just go with the flow for a while. Reflect on what you are learning about yourself while being alert to what might match up with it. If you're really stuck, talk to people who know you. Sometimes the answer is obvious when you do find it. Maybe it's just sitting there half-forgotten in your past, at a time when you did something that was fun, you did it well, and you actually got paid for it.

The only footnote I would add is this. If your search leads you forward into the future, to a business idea in a field that's new to you, it's probably not very smart to learn about it while launching your own start-up. Get some experience first. If

possible, serve an 'apprenticeship' by taking a job with another start-up or an existing company in that field. During the time you spend, you can also be preparing yourself to make the move we discuss next.

Let us take SP's example. SP was strong in math and his passion was in teaching. Many of his friends' kids would come to him for help and his friends were willing to pay him for it. When he was working in a job, all these skills were dormant. It was only when he needed to create income that he started exploring this skill as a means to earn money. The reason you need to identify your strength and passion is because an entrepreneur's journey is long and arduous and if you are doing it in the area of your strength, then you will enjoy the whole journey. You are naturally drawn to it because you want to do it and you will not quit because you are having fun. If it's a natural strength and you have a passion for it, then you have an unfair advantage that you can leverage. The other math teachers in high school did not do as well as SP as they were probably doing it because they had to do it rather than because they wanted to.

10

Changing Core Values
Types of Business

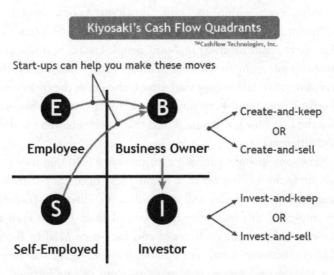

Kiyosaki's Cash Flow Quadrants

™Cashflow Technologies, Inc.

Start-ups can help you make these moves

E → B

Employee   **Business Owner**   Create-and-keep
OR
Create-and-sell

S   I

Self-Employed   **Investor**   Invest-and-keep
OR
Invest-and-sell

(The original ESBI diagram is a trademark of Cashflow
Technologies, Inc.)

Along with impacting your goals and schedule, a start-up could
call for changes in how you need to think and act. Robert
Kiyosaki's trademarked Cash Flow Quadrant model says there are
four basic occupational roles you can play in life: Employee (E),

Self-Employed (S), Business Owner (B) or Investor (I). When you begin a start-up you are initiating a move from E or S over to B, although it's also possible to invest in start-ups, as I do.

Kiyosaki notes that being in the B or I quadrant gives you the potential to make much more money. Further, he says, the people in each quadrant tend to have different *core values* in terms of their relationship to work and money. Thus, a move from one quadrant to another may require a mental adjustment as well as a change in life situation. It can take time to shift from, say, thinking like an employee to thinking like an owner.

Also, even within the same quadrant, people may have different core values depending on the type of business they choose to create or invest in. Some people create (or invest in) a start-up intending to sell their share later and make money; this is common in technology start-ups. Others take the create-and-keep or invest-and-keep approach, holding onto the business for the cash flow it provides. I find that the mentalities involved are different.

For some people, running a business in a field that they care about is the realization of a dream, and once they launch a successful start-up they will stay with it for a lifetime. (Famous examples of this mentality have ranged from Henry Ford to Gordon Moore, the co-founder and long-time head of Intel.) Others become serial entrepreneurs; they seem to thrive on the start-up process and may cash out of one business to start another.

Some see success as the chance for a midlife change, selling off their start-ups to begin a new career or take early retirement. Still others move to the I quadrant—quite a few successful entrepreneurs become angel investors or venture capitalists, putting their money and expertise into other people's start-ups—and there are some, like me, who enjoy all aspects. I

have created and sold, created and held, invested and sold and invested and held.

You will find your own path out of the many options that lie ahead. They all require cultivating certain habits and qualities of mind, which we will talk about in the last chapter of this book, 'The Mindset of an Entrepreneur'.

For now, let's turn to the qualities you need to look for in the people around you, as you build your team.

11

Finding a Mentor

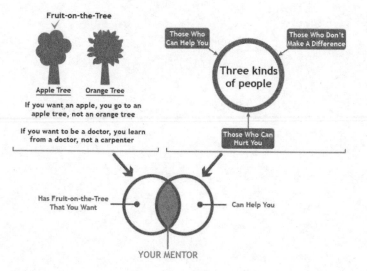

As there are many things that could go wrong in a start-up, having a mentor who has 'been there, done that' can help you avoid mistakes and increase your chance of success. But how do you find a mentor? Let's start with a couple of basic specifications.

If you want to visit and learn about a new place, you would definitely hire a tour guide who is familiar with the place, right? We call this the fruit-on-the-tree concept. Look for a mentor

who has the fruit you want, such as success in the industry you are planning to enter.

In addition, there are three kinds of people in the world, people who can help you, hurt you or don't make any difference. You want a mentor who not only has the fruit-on-the-tree, but who also is able and willing to help you (as opposed to, say, being in direct competition with your new business).

What are the benefits of having a mentor?

- Just as everyone has a blind spot while driving—an area the driver cannot see, but others can—you have blind spots in your start-up that a mentor can see.
- A mentor can help you stay focused on your objective and be persistent.
- An experienced mentor can recognize business strategies and courses of action that lead to dead ends, helping to steer your start-up in a more promising direction. And if you get off the track for any reason, the mentor can help you make corrections quickly.
- Perhaps you have some unhealthy personal traits like procrastination, a big ego or a hot temper. A good mentor can help you identify and address these shortcomings before you drive off people who are crucial to your start-up.
- A mentor can help you be accountable and get things done.

Thus, the right mentor (or mentors) can save you time, money and frustration.

A good way to start your search is by describing the type of person you're looking for. Write down the characteristics an *ideal* mentor should have. These would probably include things like knowledge of your industry (and success in it), start-up experience, and personal traits that could provide a balance or complement to your own.

Next, make a list of people you would want as your mentor, if you can think of some. Also, make a list of people who might know someone who could be your mentor. Spread the word on all your social networks. Get on the phone and start talking to as many people as possible.

If you can find a single mentor who meets all your needs, and is willing to advise you in all areas, that's great. But it's common to have more than one mentor, turning to each one for advice or support in that person's areas of strength. Another benefit is that even if somebody serves as your primary mentor, when a complex issue arises you can poll your 'committee' to get a range of viewpoints.

You don't need to pay your mentors in cash. You don't need to offer them anything at all in the beginning. Many mentors don't work out. They will drop off on their own or fade away. For the ones that stay with you and continue to add value, you can compensate them based on the value they add.

12

When and Why to Have a Co-Founder

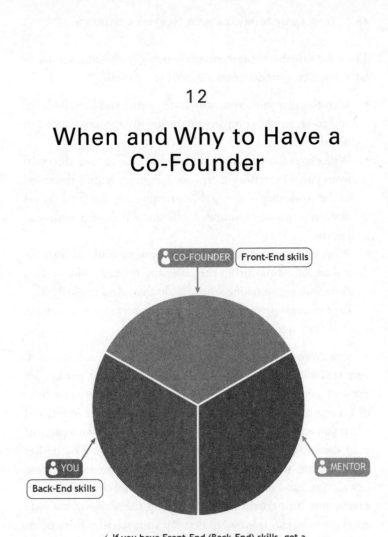

✓ If you have Front-End (Back-End) skills, get a
  co-founder with Back-End (Front-End) skills
✓ If you have both, just get a mentor

Taking on a co-founder is a crucial decision. It's different from having an assistant to whom you can delegate work, different from hiring or contracting with people for specific services.

These are valuable team members you might also add, sooner or later, but a co-founder plays a special set of roles.

- A co-founder joins you early in the game and literally helps you co-create the company by the iterative process that I will describe shortly.
- Whereas employees and contractors agree to take direction from you—exercising their own judgment within the scope of the work they're doing, but granting you the final say on any decision—a co-founder will make decisions with you jointly.
- Whereas an employee *might* be willing to work, at first, for a share of ownership in the company instead of for cash, a co-founder is someone who *will* do that. And typically it's a large enough share that the co-founder becomes a significant co-owner along with you.

So a co-founder is a person you'll need to be able to work very well with. This person will have to share your passion for the start-up, perhaps putting in a lot of time and energy for little or no compensation at the outset. That's a tall order to fill, and when you add in the fact that the co-founder will own a piece of your dream for the long term, the question arises: Why bother even looking for such a person? Some entrepreneurs choose not to. You can remain the sole proprietor and decision-maker, maybe just hiring help as needed along the way—*if you have all of the core skills required* to develop your start-up from point A ('zero') to point B ('launch'). Most of us don't, which is the main reason we look for co-founders. During the critical stages of developing and testing your offering, mentors and specialists can certainly help. But various kinds of important things have to be done well (and, often, quickly). There has to be somebody around who can do them all, in a continual and coordinated

way, bringing the pieces of the enterprise together until they shape a viable business. If you're the one, fine. Otherwise, you need a co-founder or co-founders to complete the skill set.

Typically the needed skills break out into the 'front-end' and 'back-end' kind.

Front-end skills include engaging with prospective users or customers, listening to them and observing them, to figure out what they really want or need, and how much (if anything) they are willing to pay for the solution you are offering. Then persuading them to try the solution, testing it with them, getting feedback and finally converting them to paying customers. Someone who is strong in these front-end 'people skills' might also take the lead in lining up needed partners, pitching investors on the idea and so forth.

Back-end skills include actually building and refining the solution, *along with anything needed to present it to prospects.* For instance, this might entail creation of a landing page or Slideware to explain the idea. Let's say you want to explain your idea for an email backup system. What is the best way to do that—build a PowerPoint slide? Or build a simple prototype? How soon can it be done?

People who have technology skills and can think and work smart are good back-end folks. You don't want a purist or perfectionist who wants to spend months building a solution. You need a back-end person (or people) who can quickly put something together; be willing to throw away what doesn't work; learn quickly, modify nimbly and roll out rapidly, over and over again.

In terms of 'coming to market' effectively, the heart of the Zero to Launch process is building something, putting it out there and watching prospective users interact with it. The mantra is: If you must fail, 'fail fast and fail frequently'. This allows you

to learn what users really value, so you can iteratively produce a better solution for them.

Usually one person does not have the full set of skills (or even the time and energy) to sustain this process alone, so I advise most start-ups to have a co-founding team. In a start-up I am working with currently, there are two co-founders. Let's call one co-founder Mike and the other Stan. Mike has the front-end skills. He interfaces with people, creates opt-in lists, learns by observing, etc. Stan is the back-end person, a street-smart technologist who can—within a few days—roll out successive refinements of prototypes that are testable. Mike takes a prototype, has 100 people test it, then comes to Stan with their feedback for the next iteration. Between them, Mike and Stan have a very rapid cycle of create-test-modify. It has put them on what I believe is a fast track to success.

13

Finding and Signing a Co-Founder

Once you have determined you want a co-founder, make a list of what you want from that person. What are the specific front-end or back-end skills that are needed to make your start-up successful? What type of temperament and attitude should your co-founder have? Put down as many details as you can. Do not compromise, at least not yet. Don't pick someone you know well and try to make the person fit the role. This is a big step. Cast a wide net and then be selective, not settling for less too quickly.

Make a list of all your old friends from high school or college. Also, list all the people you have worked with. Then, list the people you know who might know the kind of person you need. Look everywhere and tell everyone. Try and connect with old friends and acquaintances on LinkedIn and Facebook to help find the person who may fit the role of the co-founder. But ask, ask, ask. The key is to call as many people as you can and tell them what you are looking for.

One of the start-ups that I advise needed back-end skills. My nephew had recently graduated from a good university. So I called him and asked him (while I was asking, in parallel, a few dozen others) if he could spread the word among his friends that we were looking for an entrepreneurial type of person having

such-and-such skills. Before long, we talked to a few people he suggested and one of them turned out to be our choice.

As with finding your sweet spot, there is no one way of finding a co-founder. Hence the key continues to be persistence and spreading the word far and wide. It also helps to be flexible—whenever possible—about the location of the other person.

Many entrepreneurs I advise ask me: 'How do I know when I have found the right person?' My answer is, 'I don't know. We have to use the try-before-you-buy approach.'

When you go to buy an expensive pair of jeans, you would probably try them on first, and so it is with co-founders. I have never had anyone object to this approach. I tell the person up front that we don't know if we are a good match, so we'll try things out for a month and see what happens.

I soon realized that it's actually quite easy to find the right person. People who did not fit the role well seemed to give up quite quickly. They would be hard to reach, too busy, not interested not available and so on. In most cases they completely stopped responding or communicating and we did not even need to have a conversation about parting ways.

On the other hand, the right person stands out clearly making you think 'This is it!' That person is enthusiastic, involved, has a positive attitude, is easy to work with and in most cases fun to work with. The person also has complementary skills that balance the team and increase its overall ability to make progress.

My experience has been that it never really required a 30-day trial period. It generally took less than two or three weeks to figure out if the person would make the right co-founder.

Also, once we have worked together for a few weeks, the new co-founder knows what his role is and what our roles are, and has a good feel for the relative value everyone contributes. Thus, when it's time to discuss equity, I ask him to name a percentage

that he would be comfortable with. Some of the founders that I have shared this idea with were shocked: 'What if they ask for too much?' I have never had that problem. The co-founders have always come back with a reasonable figure.

Of course, you will want to make sure that the vesting periods are also discussed (typically four years of equal vesting). We made it clear that there will be no salary until the business is profitable and funding is raised. And we specify what the co-founder's 'lights-on' salary should be. 'Lights on' is a term my friend Krishna Pendyala uses to indicate an income level that covers bare necessities, like being able to pay bills and have lights on at home.

In summary these are the things to be agreed on: equity, when salary will start and how much. We commit this to paper as a simple one-pager and sign it.

We also warn co-founders that everyone has to live with the equity split going forward, pretty much forever. Going back after some time and trying to change equity is like unscrambling eggs and is not possible. Many other people might have joined, more shares might have been issued, the number of stakeholders might have increased and so on, thus, making it more difficult to make any changes to the equity split.

These decisions are hard to undo or redo, which means everyone has to make sure that they make the right decisions from the beginning—find the right co-founder and define the right deal.

14

The Evolution of Internet and Mobile Technologies

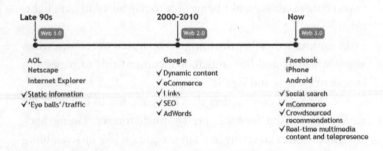

Late 90s	2000-2010	Now
Web 1.0	Web 2.0	Web 3.0
AOL	Google	Facebook
Netscape	√ Dynamic content	iPhone
Internet Explorer	√ eCommerce	Android
√ Static infomation	√ Links	√ Social search
√ 'Eye balls'/traffic	√ SEO	√ mCommerce
	√ AdWords	√ Crowdsourced recommendations
		√ Real-time multimedia content and telepresence

To this point we have been looking at your start-up mostly from the inside. You were invited to look within yourself to find inner assets, and you've seen some methods for generating a business idea and building a team.

Now let's direct our attention to what is 'out there' for a start-up to plug into—specifically in the online world. This world has evolved tremendously, making it possible to launch businesses quickly and (relatively) easily.

In the 1990s when Netscape, Internet Explorer and AOL came to the fore, people were excited about seeing websites and exchanging email. The big thrill at first was simply the ability to connect to anything that was in the new world of cyberspace.

Then we migrated to the search engine sites, culminating with Google. This was a big change because Google could do more than help you find information. It could tell you which web pages were the most important or useful on any topic. Google did this (and still does it), in part, by a form of crowdsourcing. The pages that show up highest in your search results are the ones with lots of links pointing to them from other places in the web. The assumption is that people will only link to a page if they think it's valuable. Thus, as Google likes to say, its PageRank system reflects how the global crowd of users and website operators have 'voted' on which pages are the best.

But from there we have moved on to web 2.0 and beyond. Facebook has claimed that it has 1 billion active users in December 2012. Many of them 'live' on Facebook, hardly leaving their Facebook home page except to go to other Facebook pages, or to follow links that other people on Facebook have recommended to them. And that is the leading edge of a fundamental change. Instead of using Google or other search sites, these Facebookers are sitting at 'home' and counting on friends to bring the right information to them. They no longer need surrogates for crowdsourcing—which is essentially what Google offers— *because they can crowdsource directly from the crowd.*

Other social network sites and services have emerged too, along with a parallel change, which is that people no longer connect just from a computer on a desk. They carry their connectivity everywhere on laptops, tablets, smartphones and more.

So what are the implications of all of this to you, a first-time entrepreneur? There are more platforms and channels than ever for launching new business ideas, and for testing them more widely and quickly.

You don't need to borrow a few hundred thousand dollars to buy a restaurant franchise or sacrifice 16 hours a day of your

life to run a business. Instead you could, like Ankit Gupta and Akshay Kothari, develop and test a new online business with practically no money at all. Ankit and Akshay were Stanford students when they iteratively co-created their Pulse newsreader app on an iPad by testing early prototypes with people in Palo Alto cafes!

To quote Ankit, they kept iterating until the responses went from 'This is horrible' to 'Does this come preloaded with the iPad?' Again, to quote Ankit, 'Listening to users, taking constant feedback and fearlessly iterating (even with a huge user base) has helped us a lot along the way.' The Pulse news reader not only became a top paid app in the iPhone app store, but also earned high praise from Steve Jobs, who in a keynote address called it a 'wonderful RSS reader'.

For people who say they are not technologically savvy enough to do what Ankit and Akshay did, I would ask: 'Why not find a co-founder who is?' All in all, excuses are just that, excuses. For every excuse you have, there is someone who has faced that obstacle or worse and has made it.

The Internet has a large impact on people's lives today and can be leveraged for launching new business ideas and for testing them quickly. For people who are not Internet savvy, having a co-founder who is Internet savvy or learning about the web to make an impact becomes essential.

15

Evolution of Methodologies for Creating Start-ups

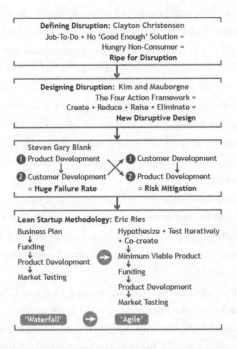

Speaking of what is 'out there' for your start-up to connect with, some very important people are out there whom you must connect with early in the game: the customers.

Many start-ups are doomed to fail, ironically, because their founders are so passionately intent upon being innovators and problem-solvers. Eager to deliver a novel solution, they assume they know the customer's problem. They plunge ahead raising and spending money to bring the product to market, only to see it crash when it finally makes contact with customers.

Worse yet, their start-up has been designed *assuming* that the product would work. Now the entrepreneurs are like deer caught in the headlights; they have burned through their funding and can only sputter in astonishment at how the 'stupid people' in the marketplace failed to understand their 'incredible breakthrough.' Funny though it may sound, this is so close to the truth that it's scary. Entrepreneurs, being die-hard, continue in a state of disbelief and denial until it's too late to save the start-up. Then an oft-repeated scene unfolds: the company cannot meet payroll, so off goes the team. The founders are unable to survive without pay, either, so they go back to jobs. The IP, if any, goes to the investors who don't know what to do with it. Nobody wins, and ideas that might have been brilliant in some other context are lost to the world.

This is why new concepts for creating start-ups have evolved, which call for focusing on and engaging with customers from the very beginning. I would like to take you on a brief journey through these methodologies; we will refer back to some of them in chapters to come.

I trace my personal journey to reading Clayton Christensen's seminal books on disruption theory: *The Innovator's Dilemma*, *The Innovator's Solution*, and *Seeing What's Next*. Here is where I started learning about hungry non-consumers—people who, as Christensen says, have a 'job-to-be-done' in their lives, but cannot find or afford a solution that satisfies them. They are non-consumers at present because they are hungry for something

that doesn't exist yet; the trick is to find these customers, identify the job and create a product to do it.

Then came W. Chan Kim and Renee Mauborgne's *Blue Ocean Strategy*, which began laying out a procedural approach for reaching those hungry non-consumers. A *blue ocean* is a wide open incipient market in which there are lots of customers and very few or no solutions (e.g., email-on-the-go when the BlackBerry first came out). In contrast, a *red ocean* is an existing market where many similar businesses are competing for the same customers. (Think of the cell phone manufacturers or the TV manufacturers with so many lookalike competitors that people almost don't care which brand they buy, so long as the price is good.) Red oceans may seem inviting because they are where the action is now, but they are 'red' with the blood of cut-throat price competition and very tough for new entrants.

In 2005, the entrepreneur Steve Blank published his book *The Four Steps to the Epiphany*, which advocated doing 'customer development' before product development instead of the other way around. Then a couple of years later, Eric Ries packaged this approach and communicated it in a way that many entrepreneurs could understand.

Ries used an analogy from the software industry. In its early days, software was developed in a straight-line sequence. You wrote requirements and specifications, then proceeded to design, coding and testing. So testing by users came last. If the program didn't work to their satisfaction or do what they wanted, you might have to go back and re-run the entire process, costing huge amounts of time and money.

Software people responded by adopting such concepts as rapid prototyping, extreme programming and agile development. These methods all include ways of involving the end users from the beginning, and co-creating the software with them

by continuous interaction and iteration. Such methods can dramatically speed up the start-to-finish cycle while reducing errors, risks and costs, and increasing customer satisfaction.

Eric Ries incorporated this thinking into what he calls 'Lean Startup Methodology.' He then started teaching the 'test early, test frequently' approach to entrepreneurs who wanted the same benefits that software engineers derive from new development methods.

Frequent iteration through customer contact has now become a major theme, and other authors have put forth their own distinct versions of it. In the 2010 book *Inside Real Innovation*, Gene Fitzgerald and Andreas Wankerl outlined a method that includes plenty of 'direct transactional experiences'—not only with customers but with prospective suppliers, partners and others, as you go iteratively down the road of developing a product and company. The goals of this 'transactional' pre-testing are *'to solicit feedback that is genuine rather than merely speculative,* and *to resolve as much uncertainty as possible with minimal commitment of one's resources or those of others.'*

By this path you can arrive at a product that really works for people, with a business that works for you. Let's continue the journey.

Wrong Approach vs Right Approach: Two Case Studies

The chart on the preceding page sums up the contrasting start-up approaches we have been talking about. We'll soon go into some depth on how to execute the 'right' approach. But first, here are a couple of case studies to illustrate the difference it can make.

To begin with something familiar, let us take SP's story and give it a different slant. Let's write a brief 'alternate history',

showing how his tutoring business might have come out if he had started with the *wrong* approach.

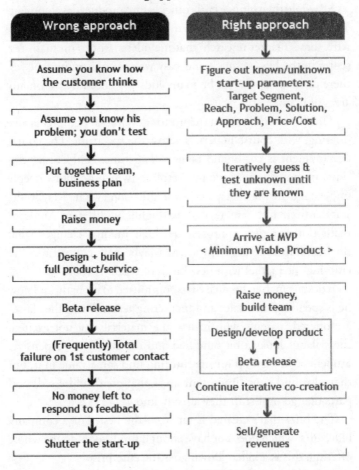

We know that SP knows a great deal about math. For this version of the story, we can imagine that he makes an unwarranted leap. Since the prospective customers for tutoring are teenagers and their parents, and since SP has been around

teenagers and parents, he assumes that he *also* knows all about what the customers need and how they think.

SP would then plunge fairly quickly into product development. To raise money he would put together a business plan, maybe with some 'market research' that includes statistics on math test scores in the US—a quick-and-easy way of confirming that yes, there certainly appear to be many kids who need help in many areas of mathematics.

Therefore, SP hires a team to develop a comprehensive offering, with course materials across the spectrum. The course development is costly and takes a long time. And during this time, it's possible that the marketplace (which he didn't deeply understand in the first place) will shift somewhat. Maybe the standardized tests are revised to highlight different kinds of math skills or new approaches, which in turn changes what the customers are eager to learn. Maybe new competitors are entering the market with new kinds of teaching tools.

It doesn't matter, because SP is committed to his path, and now he is spending on a sales and marketing team. When the classes are offered, parents who review the materials are not excited: the syllabus looks a bit outdated and the classes are expensive. Students who sign up for the tutoring find some value in it, but they also find gaps (important areas that aren't addressed) and parts that go over stuff they already know.

The buzz that's created is far from the best. For a company like Sam's, which does not have enough funds to re-do the whole offering, this is a killer. Down goes the enterprise.

And while the story you've just read is hypothetical, countless stories like it have been played out in real life, in many industries. Many of the early Internet start-ups were buried after they splurged on big but untested ideas, thinking they had to 'go big or go home'. Instead they went big AND went home.

Of course, SP in real life didn't take that approach. He started working early with some customers after first creating just a very limited set of service offerings—which, if you recall, took him 'three or four hours' to develop. Then he adapted and expanded on the fly, while teaching actual students. As the business grew he tested his assumptions with different target segments and his understanding of their problems, designing and re-designing solutions. He also experimented with the pricing and tested it along the way. The whole process was make assumptions-test-make assumptions-test-again.

SP kept repeating this until all of the parameters were known to his satisfaction and his income crossed $100,000 per year. If he wanted to build a national or global company, now would be the time to put together a business plan and raise money. His valuation would be higher as he has proven the profitability of his model, nailed down the key parameters and lowered the risk for his investors.

Now for our second case study, a true story with no hypotheticals at all.

Ramu Sunkara was an executive at Oracle when he decided to become an entrepreneur. After a few months of tinkering with 'web shows', he began to look into Internet video. That's when we met. I went on to be an advisor and an angel investor for his start-up, which was later called Qik.

Qik started off in a traditional manner. We raised money and began working on a product similar to Skype video chat. That was the wrong approach on several counts, including the fact that we were dipping into an ocean where a formidable shark, namely Skype, was already swimming.

Luckily, before going too far we asked ourselves the question: 'Who will use this product?' Then we started asking customers. Of the 100 people we surveyed, *all* of them said they were happy

with Skype video chat; they did not need another such product; and even if ours was better they would not pay for it.

So we went back to the drawing board. The Qik team came up with an idea about streaming a video from a cell-phone camera to the Internet. When we tested this idea in a survey, about 96% of the people liked it. And they said they would *use* it. In fact, they came up with 16 different use cases or situations in which they would use mobile video streaming to the Internet!

Moreover the average price they were willing to pay was $5 per month. Qik shelved the video-chat idea, drew a line, wrote off the money that was already spent and rapidly re-oriented towards this new idea. A few months later, thousands of users were tinkering with the first release of the streaming tool and Qik was able to iteratively co-create its product, in concert with the users, from there on.

By December 2010, five million people had downloaded the Qik software onto their cell phones. Also, by then, our former nemesis had re-entered the picture, except now in a friendly role. Skype bought out the company for over $100 million.

Thus, while Qik may not have gotten off on the right foot, the start-up discovered its error early enough—and then built a winning product with the help of its users.

16

Experimenting with and Testing Unknown Parameters

The process of converting unknowns to knowns by 'making assumptions and testing' is essential for nearly every start-up. Several chapters will now be devoted to exploring it further.

As we learned earlier—and as seen in the preceding table—there are six key parameters that you need to know or find out. Who are the target customers for your product or service? *Target segment* is one parameter. How to *reach* your target segment is another. Next, what is the *problem* these people have, for which they have no good solution?

The *solution* to the problem, including how to develop it, is the fourth parameter. The fifth is the *approach* for converting your target segment into paying customers. Finally, you need to know or learn what *price* the customer would be willing to pay and whether you can control the *cost* to be profitable at that price.

All of these parameters are important because they all are necessary pieces of the 'formula' for a successful business. At the start it's typical for some to be known and others unknown, so you have to develop some sort of prototype and interact with what you *think* is your target segment to start learning about the unknowns. You keep iterating and co-creating with customers until you have nailed down the whole set of parameters pretty firmly, and the pieces fit together to make a workable whole. There will be more

twists and turns ahead, but now the basics are in place well enough that you can move forward to new levels, at a higher rate.

In the language of Zero to Launch, we would say you have reached point B, true launch. In his Lean Startup Methodology, Eric Ries would say that you have arrived at your MVP: minimum viable product. Marc Andreessen simply calls this point the product/market fit.

After point B you can scale your company, grow your client base, grow your revenues and profitability and build your organization. Then you can exit by selling the company or going public, or you can keep your business running while you make positive cash flow from it.

Here are two examples of applying the six-parameter framework to an actual start-up situation. First, let us say you are a biomedical innovator. Your goal is to find a treatment for a specific type of cancer, which has resisted every treatment tried so far. That is a known problem for a known target segment, patients suffering from this cancer. How you would reach them is also known—through doctors and related channels that deal with treating cancer—and similarly, the approach runs through the same route. Price is elastic enough that you can probably set it based on cost and desired profit margin, unless the cost is so high as to be prohibitive.

The huge unknown is the solution, i.e., an effective treatment. If a satisfactory solution is found, from a business angle it's almost guaranteed to be a success.

For a second example let's choose something quite different, the email backup idea. Target segment: who needs email backup? Primarily, people who use Outlook or Outlook Express; that much is known. How do we reach them? Maybe word of mouth. Not known.

Is the problem known? Yes, people have a lot of email messages

in their inboxes, which slows down the email client. They also don't like deleting messages and they want archived messages to be easily searchable. But the solution is not known; it hasn't been designed yet. Approach is an unknown too, and so are the price and the cost.

In the cancer example, most of the parameters are known, whereas in the email example most are unknown. This illustrates a key point: the *number* of unknown parameters does not have any bearing on the degree of difficulty. Conquering the single unknown in the cancer case is likely to be the harder task by far. You are trying to succeed where many other good minds have failed, and if you should find a solution, your product will have to pass a battery of clinical trials before it ever gets to market.

	CANCER	SP	Email Backup
Target Segment	Known	Known	Known
Reach	Known	Unknown	Unknown
Problem	Known	Known	Known
Solution	Unknown	Known	Unknown
Approach	Known	Unknown	Unknown
Price/Cost	Can be determined once solution is known	Unknown	Unknown

The number of unknown parameters does, however, influence the nature of your guessing-and-testing and how you will focus it. In the cancer case nearly all of your iterating will, naturally, be focused on finding a solution. To find one without endless time, money and risk, you will want to be making highly educated guesses. In this particular field, you'll also have to test your

guesses in a prescribed sequence of ways, starting with controlled tests on cancer cells isolated in a lab. And while you can interact with the customers at any stage to get their verbal input, you won't be able to really test your solution with them until you move to the clinical trials involving real patients.

By contrast, the email backup idea calls for guessing and testing parameters all around the dial, which raises a perplexing question: Where and how do you begin? (We'll get to that.) This case is also highly amenable to (and in fact requires) engaging deeply with customers to iteratively co-create.

But as you see in the next table, regardless of which parameters are known or unknown, the goal is the same: moving them all to knowns.

For *your* start-up, you should write down what's known and what's unknown. Then you will need a plan for how to guess and test your way to point B, where they can all be put in the 'known' column. The next chapter shows how one entrepreneur did it and how another start-up could conceivably do it.

Experimenting with and Testing Unknown Parameters: The Ultimate Goal

	Point A	Point B
Target Segment	Known/Unknown	Known
Reach	Known/Unknown	Known
Problem	Known/Unknown	Known
Solution	Known/Unknown	Known
Approach	Known/Unknown	Known
Price/Cost	Known/Unknown	Known

How SP Experimented and Tested

Parameter	Point A	How did he get to 'Known' (Point B)
Target Segment	Known	
Reach	Unknown	Tested SEO, newspapers, word-of-mouth, referrals
Problem	Known	
Solution	Almost known	Improved his teaching methodology based on students' performance improvement
Approach	Unknown	Scripting & tracking what worked. Guessing, testing, adjusting.
Price/Cost	Unknown	Kept increasing price until monthly income exceeded $8,000 per month

SP went into his tutoring business with a typical mix of knowns and unknowns. His situation was also typical in the sense that known and unknown were not simple, hard-and-fast categories. Instead, the degree of 'known-ness' varied from one parameter to another, and he had to look at what it would take to turn a 'fuzzy' known into a well-defined known.

His target segment was generally known: parents of kids who were taking high school math classes and wanted to improve their grades. There were details to be learned that could lead to finer segmenting of this market, but he knew enough to make a good start.

Likewise, the problem was generally known: Improve math grades or scores. And while different kids might need different solutions, SP—with his wide knowledge of math and his ability to explain it—had a pretty good set of solutions in place, which he could draw upon and adapt without great difficulty. So the problem and solution were good-enough knowns from the start.

Now we discuss the parameters that were largely unknown: How to reach his segment through marketing, the right approach, and the right pricing?

Pricing was a classic case of iteration. Basically, SP kept increasing his prices until he met significant price resistance. In the end, he was able to get an hourly rate 'way above what he expected.' SP knew, going in, what his goals and limitations were in regard to revenue and pricing. His main goal was to make as much money as possible to support his family; his chief limitation was the number of hours he could spend tutoring: there are only so many each day. In such a case, once you see that you could fill your calendar at your current price point, why not start testing higher prices? If you're able to go high enough, you will not even need to fill the calendar in order to come out ahead.

To give a quick contrived example, suppose that SP could deliver 100 hours of tutoring at $20 per hour (for total revenues of $2,000) or 80 hours of tutoring at $40 per hour (for total revenues of $3,200). That is a no-brainer. SP, like you, would go for the $40 per hour clients, making more money with less work.

With reach and approach, SP did not theorize. He went out into the field and tested. Staying within his budget, he tried numerous things: newspaper ads, Internet SEO, word-of-mouth referrals and more. He worked directly with people, selling the service. And he kept track of what he was doing; he retained what was working and dropped what wasn't.

In the co-creative process, it's very important to learn what is working and what is not. In their book *Switch*, Dan and Chip Heath talk about 'what's working' as *brightspots*. As we guess and test unknown parameters, we want to look out for the brightspots and try to discern exactly what it's that's working. Are there common patterns? Can we build on them and create more success? More brightspots?

Experimenting with and Testing the Email Backup Idea

Now I would like to walk you through a guess-and-test process for our hypothetical email backup business. Which parameters are unknown and which are known? The problem is known (although it would never hurt to tease out as many details as we can). The solution is unknown, and has to be created.

We have a good feel for who makes up the primary target segment—MS Outlook users—but the larger segment is another unknown. We also want to learn more about the people in this segment; how they think and behave. One concept we will start using here for that purpose is the 'customer avatar,' a fictitious person representing a typical customer or type of customer within the target segment. Having this avatar in mind helps us to think of the customer as an individual rather than just a faceless member of the masses.

Finally, reach is also an unknown parameter. So are approach and price/cost.

In sum, we know there are people out there with a problem to be solved, but how do we go about turning this partly formed idea, full of unknowns, into a business? Where do we begin? This is a common situation. We have an idea but just don't know how to proceed.

The first step I would propose is to set the stage for iterative co-creation, by creating a simple website with a landing page and opt-in email capture. At this point, your landing page simply explains your value proposition to your target audience, and when people visit the site you capture their email addresses.

You will be learning a lot about your target audience, but an opening description of the customer avatar could be: 'John Smith is a busy mid-level professional in a field such as accounting. He

receives and sends about 100 email messages a day. He is afraid to delete messages in case he needs them later. He does not have time to create folders in his Outlook client and to organize his inbox. As a result, he has a few thousand email messages in his inbox and sent box. And his Outlook has been getting slower over time. To make matters worse, he does not back up his emails regularly.' You can get into greater detail (and adjust the details) as you learn.

Next you make a list of everyone you know who fits this description, plus people in your network who may know people like this. Then spread the word about emailbackup.com. You can do this through friends who will evangelize for you, as well as by going directly to prospective users. You have an attractive value proposition and all you are asking people to do, at this point, is to check it out.

Add most of your friends to your opt-in list and tell them they can opt-out if they want. Also, leave your opt-in page on your landing page. If you want to have 100 users testing the prototype versions you are going to produce, you might need 300 to 400 users on your opt-in list.

The first prototype of your email backup solution, iteration 1.0, does not even have to be a 'working' prototype. It only needs to show what the product *would* do and the features you think it should have, initially. You can start with a rapidly created visual depicting what the solution screenshot would look like. Show this to prospective users and get their feedback. See who is showing the most interest and then fine-tune your customer avatar description based on that.

Now pick one or two features that were most commonly liked or commented upon in your visual prototype. Build a barely working prototype. Again go back to about 100 users, asking them to use this prototype and give feedback. Then you iterate

back and forth until you have nailed down the key features that users definitely want and like.

After that you probably test the price. And you might test various partner channels until you find the right reach. Approach is solidified based on brightspot analysis of sales. When all parameters are known, and more and more people are using the product, you are at point B. You are launched.

This happy story, however, gives just a very brief overview of some important steps in the process. There are more points to be considered, some of which are fine points that can make a big difference.

17

Determining the Problem

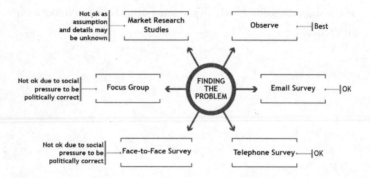

One place where details can matter immensely is in determining and defining the customer's problem. To provide a good solution to a problem, you have to know that one exists and know its nature, including the sub-problems that can arise on the way to solving it.

And getting input from customers can be tricky. In developing an idea for an email backup system, for instance, you will be 'competing with' what customers already do for that purpose. To learn the nature of the competition, you might ask people some questions like these:

- How do you back up your email right now?
- What do you like about how you do it?

• What do you not like about your current approach?

Some people may say they simply back up their entire email directly on an external hard drive. They like the fact that it's easy to do; maybe they do not like the fact that it's hard to retrieve specific messages in case there is a crash and they lose their Outlook emails.

Others will say they don't bother with backup. Those who use Gmail may say they don't have a problem to begin with, as they never run out of space, and so forth. You are learning (or confirming) important points, and you can *probably* trust that people's answers are accurate and reliable in this case.

Asking is only one way of getting information, however, and it's not always sufficient. When you are asking, the person's conscious mind is answering your question. But when a person is doing, the subconscious mind is doing by habit. What the conscious mind answers and what the subconscious mind does could be entirely different.

Furthermore, when you start asking people about some new product they *might like to have* or something they *would or would not want to do* in the future—as opposed to what they're doing right now—relying on what they say can be very misleading.

For example, suppose you were an early MP3 player inventor. If you had asked people, 'Would you like a portable device that you can transfer digital music to, and play?', most people would probably have said 'yes.' Then later on, you started selling MP3 players and they never took off, whereas the iPod, which was based on the same technology, came along and was a runaway success.

How did that happen? In the case of the early MP3 players, there was poor communication in the marketing, compounded by some sub-problems that were not uncovered until it came to actually using the product.

1. The early players were marketed as having '256 megabytes of memory'. No one understood what this meant.
2. There were issues about piracy of music. Record labels at that time were suing the digital tune-sharing company called Napster, and many people were afraid of having anything to do with downloading music and carrying it around.
3. Even if you managed to get some music onto your computer, you needed an advanced degree to transfer it to your MP3 player.
4. If you succeeded in doing that, you would need another advanced degree beyond the first one to select the music and play it.

Apple, with the iPod, quickly overcame the marketing—communication hurdle. Instead of offering megabytes of storage the company offered '25,000 songs in your pocket'. I can understand that! Apple headed off the piracy issue by creating iTunes first, which made digital music legal to download and also made it more cost-efficient to buy, since instead of having to buy a whole CD you could pick your favourite tracks for 99 cents each.

Finally, the company's famous attention to usability made it easy to transfer, select and play music with the iPod. The click-wheel interface was not only intuitive but habit-forming. In all of these matters, the company had gotten a great understanding of how people 'use' music—and how an MP3 player could enable them to use it enjoyably anywhere.

Such an understanding comes from knowing how to get multiple forms of customer input. Along with listening to what people say, you have to *observe* what they do.

18

Observing

'Actions speak louder than words.' Simply observing people can reveal problems, needs and market opportunities that otherwise might be neglected.

Let us rewind the clock to the days when MapQuest was a hot item. The Internet was still relatively new, and millions of people accustomed to finding directions from paper maps were learning about the MapQuest website. Instead of having to trace out routes and guess which of several routes might be the best, they could simply type in their starting and destination addresses. MapQuest would instantly give them the fastest route along with step-by-step directions that they could print and take with them.

Imagine that you had the idea for the next-generation improvement—GPS on board the vehicle—and you wanted to test the market. If you went to a 100 drivers and did a survey, the Q and A might have gone something like this:

'What do you use for directions currently?'

'MapQuest.'

'How do you like it?'

'It's incredible.'

'What do you not like about it?'

'Nothing. I am fine with it.'

'If we could make something better, something you could have installed right in your car, would you want it?'

'Not really. I am perfectly happy with MapQuest.'

But if, instead of asking them, you watched people as they used MapQuest, you would start noticing some common patterns.

- Sometimes they print out directions and leave them at home. Then they have to go back for the printout, or find their way by some other means.
- When they are travelling alone, they try dangerous tricks like holding the directions on the steering wheel so they can read them while driving.
- If they take a wrong exit and get lost, the MapQuest directions are no help. They may have to stop and ask.

Why don't customers tell you about these problems? The steps they are taking to compensate are called patches or workarounds. When people encounter challenges in using a product, they come up with patches to make them work. Over time those patches become habits, so they don't think about them anymore, and, therefore, don't mention them or even consciously recall doing them in many cases.

Products also have limitations that cannot be overcome, but people may not mention those either, for much the same reason—they have gotten used to living with the limitations. That is why it pays to observe users in action.

For those of us involved with the Qik start-up, it paid off hugely. In 2006, the Qik team observed people taking videos with camcorders. Since the camcorders were too bulky to fit in a pocket, people often didn't have them along when an unexpected video opportunity arose. And videos that were taken with camcorders tended to sit in the machines for months. People thought it was a huge task to transfer their videos to a computer and then upload

them to YouTube or Facebook. These observations helped lead Qik to the business idea that took off for the company: providing

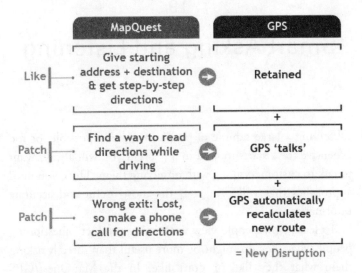

technology to stream video from cell phone cameras to the Internet, skipping the intermediate steps.

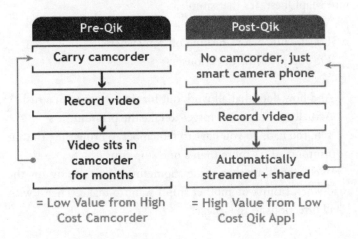

19

Smart Asking and Listening

Observing a large sample of people may be impossible, or too expensive for a start-up, and in any event you will always want to talk to customers along with observing them. Thus, you need approaches that will bring out the most useful and accurate information.

To learn how people view an existing product, questioning people what they do might be more useful than directly asking them what they like or don't like. In the MapQuest/GPS example, suppose you had asked people to describe how they use MapQuest. You might hear something like, 'I put the address into MapQuest. It's that simple.'

'When do you do that?'

'Usually just before rushing off somewhere.'

'Do you print the directions?'

'Yes.'

'And how does that all work out for you, if you're in a rush?'

'Actually, sometimes I forget to take the printout.'

'Oh, too bad. So you have to remember to bring the printout or printouts, if it's more than a one-stop trip?'

'Well, that's another thing. Sometimes I'm already on the road when I think of another stop I want to make. Then I wish I had directions to that place!'

You make a note of these challenges and check with other users to learn if they are common ones. Similar detailed questioning might bring out the challenge of reading a printout while driving alone or having to get new directions when you take a wrong exit.

Question-asking is often done in a survey format, and there multiple ways of conducting surveys: by phone, in person, by email or online. Of these, phone tends to be the best. You can get a personal, interactive feel for the customers without literally getting 'in their face', which may create subtle pressure for them to give answers that will 'save face.'

Another important point here is that focus groups do not work. People do not say what is on their minds. They will often simply agree with others in order not to offend, or they will say what they think comes off as 'correct' in some other sense. As a result wrong information is gathered, wrong problems are identified and solved, and no one wants the solution when it's delivered.

To test the problem, solution or any other parameter by asking and listening:

- Write down a clear description of the 'customer avatar' you will be talking to.
- How many people do you want to test: 100? 1,000?
- What questions do you have in mind? Remember that the questions you choose, and how you phrase them, will influence the answers you get.

Next we will consider a very powerful way of communicating with customers verbally: by creating and telling stories.

20

Using Use Cases (a.k.a. 'Stories')

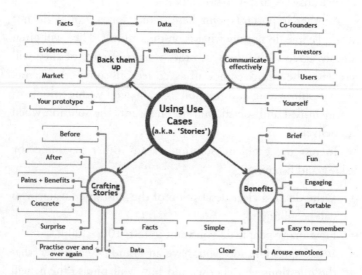

Over the years, one of the best ways I have found to discover problems or test our products is to express them succinctly to the people we deal with—be they prospective customers, investors or co-founders—by using *use cases or stories*.

The term 'use cases' was coined by Ivar Jacobson, a computer scientist. A use case is simply a story that describes how a person

would use a product, for a particular purpose. Jacobson saw that writing stories of this type was a great way to spell out specifications to software engineers creating a new program. You were essentially telling them: 'Okay, here's what people will want to be able to do with the software, so be sure to make it so they can do that'—and when it was put in that form, the software engineers could really get it.

Similarly, people of all kinds will really get what you are trying to convey when you tell them a typical user's story. They will see the problems, the solutions, the benefits of the product; they'll be able to relate to the story and give you highly relevant feedback.

People love to hear stories because stories bring the situation to life. Going back to our example of the email backup system, suppose you are building the system and you want to get the benefits across to a prospective customer. Here are a couple of stories you could tell.

Story 1: If you are a regular email user, you have an email client and you download email messages. You probably get 50 messages a day and you probably send out 20. You have a few thousand messages in your inbox and a slightly smaller number in your sent box. And your email client has become so slow that it irritates you to start up. (This is a good place to pause and have the other person respond, usually in agreement).

Now imagine you have a new backup system that ensures that all your email is auto-magically backed up, except for the last seven days. But even that is seamlessly available to you if you want any of it. And your email client runs like a race horse. How would you like that? Would you use something like that? Would you pay for it?

Story 2: You are a regular email user and you have thousands

of messages in your inbox and sent items. You are searching for the email ID of somebody, and it's a real pain. The other day, you were searching for some attachment that was sent to you last year, a really important document that you can't find at all. Maybe it vanished when the computer crashed. Maybe you backed it up, but you have no idea how to retrieve it. Does any of this sound familiar?

Now imagine you have a new backup system that you can search using Google's search engine. You want to find an attachment? It has indexed all of them. It intelligently learns all your contact information and synchronizes it with your iPhone contacts, so you can get hold of anybody by any method, email, or phone or driving over to their street address. Would you like that? Would you pay for something like that? How much?

There are many advantages of telling stories:

- Stories speak in the user's language. You are not using the 'builder's language' of the kind of engine and chassis and high-tech steering and suspension systems you have put into a new automobile. You are telling people about the fantastic pickup and smooth ride they're going to get, and how this car handles on tight curves like a dream.
- Stories travel. The listener tends to remember stories easily and pass them on to others.
- Stories are modifiable. You can tailor them to speak about the aspects of your product that will resonate with the listener's own experience.
- Stories are fun. People pay attention and listen.
- Stories paint pictures. Often such pictures are emotional, which brings home the situation you are describing and magnifies the benefits of your proposed solution.

- Stories simplify and they're brief. Sometimes, you can communicate in a few minutes what would take you hours using explanations and abstractions.

So construct stories and keep modifying them as you learn more and more from the market. Improve them. Use them daily with your prospective investors, users, co-founders and employees. *Use them with yourself*, to understand your target segments and their problems, and to communicate effectively with them.

Here are some techniques for constructing stories:

- 'Before and after' is a classic story structure. *Here's how the email experience is before using our backup system…and here's what it's like after you get the system.*
- 'Pains and benefits' is a theme that needs to be emphasized. *These are the pains you encounter when you don't use our system (slow email client, difficulty backing up and retrieving)…and these are benefits you enjoy when you use it (now you can search attachments at the speed of Google, etc.)*
- Make stories concrete by using names. 'Sarah uses Outlook Express' is better than 'a person uses an email client.'
- Surprise people. Put in story elements or ways of saying things that convey benefits in an eye-opening way. If someone at Skype, when it was founded, told you your international phone bill could be 'a big fat zero', you would probably listen!
- Practise over and over again. With your cat, with your spouse, with your neighbour, with your mirror, with anyone, really, who is crazy enough to stand still and listen.

Back up your stories with real data. Use interesting and relevant numbers. 'We talked with 100 people and 96 of them

liked our idea. They even gave us use cases; we came out with 16 distinct use cases. And, on the average, they were willing to pay $5 per month.'

Bottom line: use stories. They cost nothing and they are worth their weight in gold.

21

Talking about Your Own Problems

Finding out what people like or dislike about current products is one way of determining their problems and designing the right solutions. But there could be many small problems that are hindering you from designing the right solution, or from running your business. Talking to others about these problems can often point you to the solutions, or to ways to find them.

I had a friend who suffered from acute chronic pain in the alimentary canal. His doctors had been giving him steroids, which were not effective, so we were discussing what to do. Out of some random insight I said, 'I don't think the doctors can help you. They are not motivated; they are not going through the pain! You need to find someone who had the same problem as you. Search on the Internet for someone who has cured himself, or herself, and do what that person did.'

After this, I forgot about the conversation. Then a week later my friend came back and told me he was feeling better. When I asked how this had happened, he said, 'I followed your advice.' He had found someone with the same condition, who had been in remission for two years. What worked in that case was a natural dietary remedy, eating a certain kind of seeds. My friend

said 'I took the seeds and my pain, which was a 10 on a scale of 1 to 10, is now a 1.'

I asked him, 'What seeds are these?' He said, 'They are called Chia seeds. They were used by the native Americans. They used them for endurance, for better digestion, for health and all kinds of things. I never would have heard about these seeds on my own, never would have tried them, or if I did it would have taken me a 100 years.'

I would give the same advice to an entrepreneur. Find another entrepreneur who has done what you want to do and succeeded multiple times. Make that person your advisor and follow his or her advice.

In the same way that we get ideas by observing and talking with users, we can get them by discussing our problems with people who have solved such problems. So long as we don't overrate the ideas and we are using our common sense, it's a productive exercise.

Finding ideas is great, but evaluating them is important. The next chapter brings out some points to consider in trying to be sure that we don't implement bad ideas—or miss the chance to implement good ones!

22

Beware...

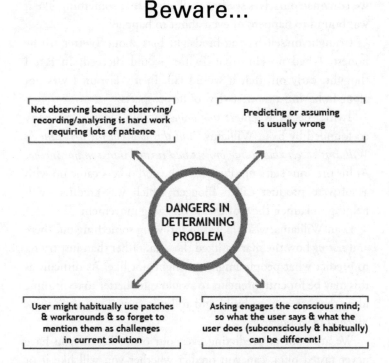

Not observing because observing/
recording/analysing is hard work
requiring lots of patience

Predicting or assuming
is usually wrong

DANGERS IN
DETERMINING
PROBLEM

User might habitually use patches
& workarounds & so forget to
mention them as challenges
in current solution

Asking engages the conscious mind;
so what the user says & what the
user does (subconsciously & habitually)
can be different!

Nassim Taleb in his book *Fooled by Randomness* warns us not to overestimate the value or correctness of our knowledge. Among other things, he talks about the biases we are subject to, many of which can be quite dangerous for entrepreneurs.

For example, if we dwell mainly on our own experiences and viewpoints, we're liable to think we can predict the future. We might think it will unfold just like something we've seen in the past, or think we've spotted an important trend that nobody else

has noticed. (When in fact, maybe others are paying it no notice because it's not important at all.)

Conversely, cases of *hindsight bias* are very common. We didn't know that a particular event would happen, but afterward we convince ourselves we knew all along that something like it was bound to happen, or even about to happen!

I caught myself having hindsight bias about Twitter. To be honest, I had no clue that Twitter would succeed. In fact I thought, early on, that it would fail. In my favour, I was not alone in having a modest view of its prospects.

Twitter began as a mere *side project* within Odeo, a company co-founded by Evan Williams. *And this was not the first time in Williams' career that a side project had turned into a major success.* At his previous start-up, Pyra Labs, he and others came up with a software product called Blogger, which was credited with helping to launch the worldwide blogging movement.

Evan Williams' wisdom was in throwing something out there and *testing* how the market liked the idea, rather than just trying to predict what people might or might not like. As difficult as this may be for entrepreneurs to swallow, it's better to test simple ideas that are easy to build and roll out *even if you don't think much of them yourself!*

We are poor at predicting even our own likes. If you have never tasted okra, can you predict whether you will like it or not? Unlikely! And if we cannot forecast what will be a hit with ourselves, maybe we should predict others' likes even less and test more.

If we are to take the movie *Social Network* as an accurate rendition of the true story, then Mark Zuckerberg simply put out a low-cost bet. He essentially bet that he could build—inebriated—a Harvard hot-or-not application. Within a few weeks he built the first version of Facebook and rolled it out. The

rest of it was then a test–learn–refine process: Facebook would test a new feature to see how people liked it and used it, and based on this feedback the founders either retained, discarded or modified the feature.

If you aren't sure whether an idea will work, make a low-cost bet. Build a prototype quickly and cheaply, then roll it out for testing.

23

Analysis of Data

Factors in How Customers Do Their 'Job' Now

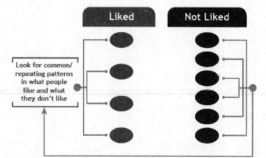

Look for common/repeating patterns in what people like and what they don't like

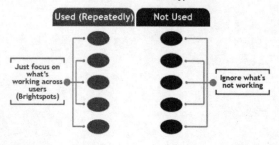

Features of Your Prototype

Just focus on what's working across users (Brightspots)

Ignore what's not working

You have rolled out a prototype, done your testing, and gotten some data and feedback from the users. How do you analyse the results?

First, consider a human tendency we need to keep in mind. I have tried this with several audiences: If there is a whiteboard in the room, and I put a black dot on it with a marker and ask the people what they see, majority will say, 'A black dot.' They say this even though the white space is much, much bigger! It's a rare person who says, 'I see a whiteboard.'

So be careful about analysing 'outliers' in your data. If you get an occasional comment or result that stands out from the rest, it might be a clue to something valuable—like a new use for the product, or a problem you hadn't thought of—but don't let it distract you from the big picture that's emerging.

Another thing we tend to do is to over-learn. We are like the cat that sat on a hot stove. After that it will not sit on any stove, hot or cold. The subconscious mind is inherently protective. It tends to seek out potential negatives or dangers in the environment and constantly, automatically tries to keep us away from these negatives.

What should you focus on, then, when looking at feedback from your customers? There are a number of sources that all suggest the same thing. Focus on the positive, focus on what's working: the brightspots, as Chip and Dan Heath call them.

Whenever you notice recurring brightspots in your data, you want to delve deeper into them. Try to learn *why* the product or feature is working, and for what kinds of customers, and what they are using it for. As you learn, you can start fine-tuning your product as well as your understanding of who comprises the target segment.

Brightspots do not have to be huge and dazzling; they just have to recur often enough to be significant. If you test a prototype with five people and no one likes it that may not mean much because your sample size is very small. But if 3 out of 100 like it, that's 3% and it could represent a big market niche for you to

capture, if the idea scales across a billion people on the Internet. Also, look at how the various features and benefits are regarded. Keep what people like and drop what they don't, then go back and re-test.

This can be done by A/B testing, in which 'A' is the control version of your product—the current baseline version—and 'B' is the product with a significant variation or addition. A/B testing properly done in conjunction with brightspot analysis can help you converge on an MVP: minimum viable product.

24

The Power of Brightspot Analysis
Jerry Sternin's Story

A major part of the business consultant's job involves analysing a lot of data. If we were launching a new marketing technique or a new feature, we would examine the statistics that would indicate how successful the feature or marketing technique was. We would probably find that 10 people are using the new feature and 90 aren't. The traditional tendency was to focus on those 90 people and figure out why they are not using the feature. This is the common tendency that I have observed among people.

The first time this methodology was completely reversed in my mind was when I read about it in a book called *Influencer: The Power to Change Anything* by Kerry Patterson et al. I read about a guinea worm disease in Africa and how it had spread to many countries. The traditional methodology was reversed here and they tried to find out why the guinea worm disease had left certain places untouched. Statistically, they said that this was a positive deviation from the norm. The study revealed that the simple practice of using a cloth filter before pouring water into a mud pot ensured that the larvae of the guinea worm did not enter people's systems and, therefore, these places were disease free. This practice was then recommended with some

other refinements and they managed to control and eradicate the disease. That was the first time I heard of the story about positive deviances.

I came across the concept of positive deviances again in *Switch*, which is a book written by the Heath brothers. There was a story about Jerry Sternin and his wife Monique who arrived in Vietnam in 1990 after their employer, the non-profit group Save the Children, had been invited in by the Vietnamese government. The task was to improve the health of children throughout the country via better nutrition. This was not only a gigantic public health problem but also a social problem, as any solution might have to involve changes in everything from food supplies to eating habits. When Jerry landed he was told that he had *six months* to make a difference. Fortunately, Jerry and Monique were so constrained by the language barrier, lack of money and lack of time that they were forced to think out of the box. They started looking for children in the lower socioeconomic strata of Vietnam who appeared to be well nourished and healthy, then tried to discover what these kids and their families were doing. In short, they studied the brightspots.

They found out that the healthier kids were hand fed by the mothers atleast four times a day. They were being fed the same amount of food but since the kids had smaller stomachs, they decided to spread it across more meals. And while most children in Vietnam normally did not eat when they were sick, these kids were encouraged to eat even when they were feeling unwell. Finally, the healthiest children were eating a variety of foods, including shrimp, sweet potatoes, greens and other foods that were considered 'low-class'. These were widely available as cheap or even free additions to the diet. Jerry realized that these methods were easy to duplicate and scale as they did not involve additional cost.

Moms of healthy kids became teachers. They were taught what to teach and how to, and they taught by showing not telling. Six months later, positive changes were definitely under way, and surveys after two years revealed that malnutrition rates had been reduced by 85%.

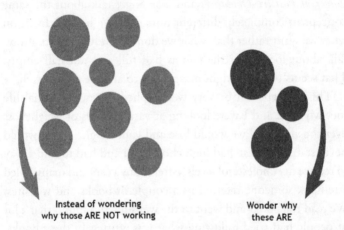

Instead of wondering
why those ARE NOT working

Wonder why
these ARE

As I learnt the impact of positive deviances, I started using this in various parts of my own life. During the early stages of my involvement in Qik, a lot of people would sign up for Qik, but there were very few people left at the end of 90 days. That's when I decided to use this opportunity to look at positive deviances in the data and understand why and how certain people had been using the service for the entire period of 90 days.

We found that as soon as these people downloaded Qik, they would create a video and share it with a couple of friends. That aspect of immediately creating a video and sharing it with friends was a key observation. This observation helped us come up with a variety of techniques to make sure that Qik was easy to download and easy to share with friends. This made the application much more sticky and successful.

The Secret is another book that talks about how you need to focus your attention on what you want and not what you don't want. It's like telling a child 'Don't break the toy'—the only picture it creates in the mind of the child is that of the broken toy. Brightspot analysis from the Heath brothers, *The Power of Positive Deviances* and *The Secret* talk about the same concept in completely different domains. We have to focus on what we want rather than what we don't want. Optimists always talk about looking at the cup as half full and not half empty. That seems to be the right perspective to analyse data as well.

This concept can be very well applied to your personal life too. My wife and I were looking at various ways of weight loss over the years and we would lose and gain weight, but it would never stabilize. I also had high cholesterol and had to find a way to reduce my cholesterol levels. After many years and many failed attempts, someone referred us a couple of books and websites. We read the books and went to the websites and found that a lot of people had tried following what was written in these books. There were a lot of testimonials and videos and medical doctors explaining why most diets did not work and what worked. We also started gathering a handful of techniques that made these kind of things work for others. Here are some of the insights we gained.

- They did not go grocery shopping when they were hungry because that's when one is likely to buy chips and ice cream.
- They always went out with a shopping list that ensured that they bought only those things that were on the shopping list.
- The more disciplined of the two should go shopping, in my case, it was my wife and I would generally wait in the car.
- If it's not at home, it's not in the stomach.

We started noticing that we began violating some of the rules when we went out and ended up eating a lot of cheese and cream. We found that the couples generally had a list of where they would order and what they would order at least for the frequently visited restaurants. We ensured that we had a set of three or four options so we would know exactly what to order at the places we frequented. These are things we learnt from others and we copied them.

If there was a breakdown, we tried not to freak out and treated the bad days as good data to see how these situations can be avoided in the future. So we applied brightspots in a business setting and in a personal setting. Over the last year and a half between my wife and I, we dropped about 32 pounds and my cholesterol level is under 150, which is supposed to be healthy. I am healthier now than when I was half my age! Consider brightspot analysis a key tool to add to your toolkit when you set out to co-create a winning product along with your team members and prospective customers.

25

Living with Black Swans

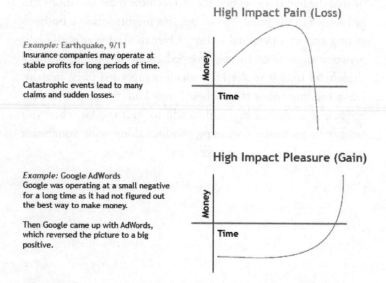

High Impact Pain (Loss)

Example: Earthquake, 9/11
Insurance companies may operate at
stable profits for long periods of time.

Catastrophic events lead to many
claims and sudden losses.

High Impact Pleasure (Gain)

Example: Google AdWords
Google was operating at a small negative
for a long time as it had not figured out
the best way to make money.

Then Google came up with AdWords,
which reversed the picture to a big
positive.

The concept that Nassim Taleb is best known for writing about
is the black swan. Black swans are rare events of high impact,
and they can be either negative or positive.

The insurance industry, for example, is prone to negative
black swans. Insurance companies are designed to make steady,
predictable profits, but they can be hit hard by claims when a
major disaster occurs. Along with its many tragic effects, the

9/11 attack caused the highest total of 'insured losses' of any catastrophic event to that time.

On the other hand, the publishing industry is prone to positive black swans. Once in a while, out of the blue, an unheralded first-time author writes a book that becomes a runaway best seller.

The world of start-ups is prone to *both* kinds. Entrepreneurs worry that some unexpected event will wipe out their fragile ventures—maybe a sudden shift in the market, or a new move by a competitor—while with the other half of their brains, they keep hoping to strike upon the Next Big Thing.

Is there any way to lower the risks of being devastated by a negative black swan? Or to increase your odds of coming across a positive one? Indeed there is a way to do both, and it's the strategy I mentioned earlier: making low-cost bets and testing them.

If you place a high-cost bet on an idea that hasn't been tested very well, you incur a risk beyond the risk that the idea might not work. You are making yourself more vulnerable to unexpected shocks. The little boat of your start-up can get so weighed down with expenses and debts that a wave of bad luck might swamp it, whereas a more nimble boat might have a shot at riding out the storm.

Furthermore, 'testing the waters' with low-cost bets over a wide area can help you find your way to the prize. Google, in its early years, struggled to find a revenue model that would make the company profitable. Several were tried until a fairly simple one, AdWords, turned out to be a big winner. Although there is no guarantee that you will reap such a bonanza, you can follow the same sort of path to home in on something that works.

The trick, for you, is to keep your bets as close to zero cost as you can while iteratively co-creating to converge on a profitable

business model. You are in a race between the time needed to converge and the money (and human persistence) needed to keep placing low-cost bets until convergence happens. Start-ups fail when either the entrepreneurs lose their fire and stop persisting, or when they run out of money.

What I am saying about low-cost bets may sound contrary to conventional wisdom. Some people think that in order to hit it big, you have to be a high-stakes gambler with a 'no guts, no glory' attitude—making bold moves and committing totally to your ideas, then sticking with them until you do or die. But that is mistaking pig-headedness for persistence. It also gets you into a psychological trap, because once you invest heavily in a flawed idea, it becomes harder to cut your losses and move forward.

What you have to commit to is your ability to create value for customers. They are the people who will decide whether you have a black swan, a turkey or something in between.

The Four Actions Framework
from *Blue Ocean Strategy*®

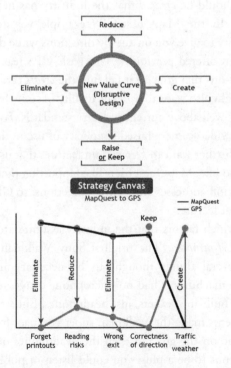

Here is a strategic approach for developing products and services that will stand out from the offerings currently available to your customers.

Formulated by W. Chan Kim and Renee Mauborgne, the Four Actions Framework is similar to Clayton Christensen's disruption theory. Both are useful for creating a disruption or harvesting a blue ocean—a target segment of un-served or under-served customers; the hungry, non-consuming kind that we have talked about.

The Four Actions are *Create, Raise or Keep, Eliminate* and *Reduce.* They work together to establish a new 'value curve' for the target segment.

1. What should be *created* that the industry has never offered before? In the MapQuest/GPS example we studied, the capability to give you on-the-fly directions while driving had not been offered previously. This basic GPS feature and all the add-ons that go with it fall into the *create* category.

2. You might also want to *raise* the quality of some features and benefits well above current industry standards. For example, the flip video camera raised simplicity of use noticeably. We would further want to *keep* certain features that users already have and like. MapQuest users liked inputting their start and destination addresses and getting directions, so GPS systems kept that feature.

3. Now, which factors that the industry assumes are necessary can be *eliminated?* The original Sony Walkman did away with several things thought to be necessary in portable cassette machines It had no microphone or recording heads and no built-in speakers, just headphones! But stripping out these items made the Walkman super-compact for listening to music on the go, and even the headphones-only feature turned out to be a plus: you could listen in public without disturbing others or having their noise disturb you.

4. Finally, which factors can be *reduced* well below the industry

standards? Southwest Airlines, when it launched, found ways of reducing airfares well below what others were charging.

We can use the Four Actions to draw a strategy canvas. The preceding graphic shows how the GPS strategy improved upon MapQuest (and suggests why GPS came to be the new standard). Of course, as you make Four-Actions changes you will need to keep testing them to see if they indeed reflect what customers want. But if you arrive at a product that delivers a substantially new value curve, you are likely to have the makings of a substantial success.

27

Geoffrey Moore's
Crossing the Chasm

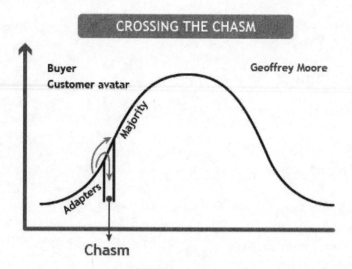

A product that tests well may draw some eager early adopters, but there are relatively few of these customers. The 'early majority' are those who will—it's hoped—come aboard next, making your company profitable while giving your product a growing, critical-mass presence in the marketplace. And between the two groups lies a chasm to be crossed. Most start-ups cannot afford

to mass-market to the early majority; they are likely to run out of money before they get to profitability.

So instead, Geoffrey Moore suggests that you try and find a niche (a 'first bowling pin') in which you offer a compelling reason to buy your product. Iteratively co-create a whole product for that niche. Dominate the niche while simultaneously moving to profitability. Then, by a domino effect, knock down neighbouring 'bowling pins' or niches and keep growing. For example, presumably it was this kind of iteration that helped BlackBerry move from being an email-only device to an email-plus-phone device.

This fits with our Zero to Launch framework because we recommend an early definition of your customer avatar or buyer persona. The customer avatar not only clearly represents your target segment, but also helps you stay focused on the target segment long enough to get to point B and beyond (to sustainable and growing profitability).

One famous example of a company crossing the chasm and going from stagnant revenues to rapidly multiplying revenue streams is Documentum. The company, founded in 1990 as a maker of business software for managing documents and content, was posting annual revenues of only around $2 million when Jeff Miller took over as CEO in 1993.

Instead of trying to grow revenue across the board, Miller picked a target segment that was going through great difficulty in preparing and managing documents. The people in this chosen segment worked at pharmaceutical companies. Every time a company develops a new drug, it has to get regulatory approval to come to market. This means submitting a document called a New Drug Application in the US, and/or its equivalent in other countries.

If you want to market worldwide you may have to file

applications with 100 or more regulatory bodies in different countries. A single application can run to as long as 500,000 pages. It was taking companies nearly a year to file, which was costly not only in terms of the expenses involved, but in terms of income lost. The filing process begins only after patents have been awarded—typically for 17 years, so the revenue clock is ticking—and during this time an average drug may earn over $400 million per year. Thus, every day spent on applications was costing more than a million.

Documentum provided a solution that cut filing time dramatically. And once the software had helped to solve problems within this specific, high-profile niche, many other firms in industries with similar problems began to approach Documentum. The bowling pins toppled one after another as the product spread to chemical companies, oil refineries, property leasing firms and even Wall Street. Before long, Documentum had pulled itself across the chasm, realizing annual revenues of about $75 million.

The story is relevant for all entrepreneurs because the executive council that is funding the start-up needs to be able to see beyond the first niche to the extended market, and understand the product's full potential. However, if the total market is shown to funders directly, the expectations and pressures may be unrealistic and difficult to realize. So the approach has to be clearly explained and worked on—with a focus on the immediate niche at present, and a view towards growing into other markets eventually.

28

Habits and Virality

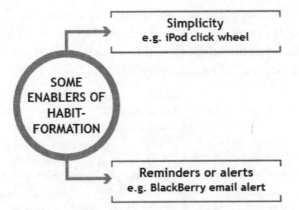

We've learned that co-creating a product with users can increase our chances of success while reducing costs and risks.

During the co-creation process, however, we have to pay attention to another thing besides user feedback and iteration. Are the prospective users signing up and trying our product just once, then vanishing? Or are the same people coming back repeatedly? In other words, is the use of our product or service becoming a habit?

Ensuring that usage becomes habit-forming is not only a smart move, it's essential. Without it, your start-up will fail. The early MP3 players, pre-iPod, were so hard to use that people could

not grow 'accustomed' to them—making their use a custom, or habit—which was a big reason they died. The iPod's click wheel, on the other hand, was easy to use and quickly habit-forming. Similarly, the BlackBerry had an alert that went off each time a new email was downloaded. You were literally being 'prompted' to check your new message—promptly! This alert made the BlackBerry more than habit-forming. It became such an addiction that the users were called Crackberries.

Thus, we can learn at least two factors that promote habit formation: simplicity or ease of use, and alerts or reminders during the usage process. Can you think of others? Start noticing products you use habitually, and think about what it is that has made them part of your everyday life.

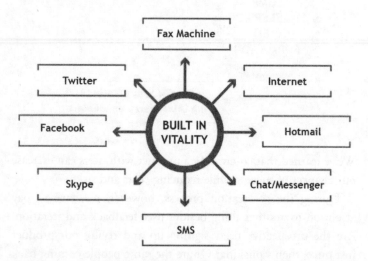

Another force you want to tap, closely related to habit formation, is virality. Viral growth of the user base for your product is important for two reasons: it dramatically decreases the customer acquisition cost, and it feeds on itself. As viral growth progresses, the number of people who are *interconnected*

by use of your product increases—which, in turn, leads even more people to want to use it. This is called the 'fax effect.' When fax machines were introduced, it would have been pointless to be the only person in the world who had one. But as more and more people began to use them, the value of having a fax machine increased. Eventually, at least in the world of business, it became a necessity.

The same sort of thing has happened with Facebook, Skype, Twitter, Hotmail, Chat and SMS. However, as noted earlier, I believe Facebook is different. Whereas people would use a fax machine for a specific purpose and then move on to other things, they tend to 'live' on the Facebook network and use it for many purposes.

The number of Google searches is coming down, and surfing the rest of the web is also decreasing, as Facebookers stay in their network and rely on it to provide them with all sorts of things—from needed information to notes and quotes to recommendations and links. Even more types of web functions may soon be migrating to this network: Where will people buy and sell things? On Facebook. Recruit and job-hunt? Ditto.

Bringing products and services that people have used in the Google world into the new Facebook world thus becomes a great business opportunity. Facebook provides a backbone that makes it easier to spread a good idea virally. Unlike the cases in which interconnections have to be created for each new product or service, Facebook has 'hardwired' the interconnections, so that if you pass 'electricity' through the wires, it lights up the entire network instantly. While this may be somewhat of an exaggeration at present, it's growing closer to the truth. We will see many new products growing virally on Facebook, faster than anything we have seen before.

You may ask: but how do we know that Facebook itself will be around for the long term? Naturally there is no guarantee. Many companies that once were household names are now gone. Entire technologies are displaced, just as faxing has been displaced, in many homes and offices, by the practice of scanning and sending paper documents as pdf files.

Yet even if Facebook, the company, were to stumble and fade away, or if some of the enabling technologies were to change, the 'Facebook world' that I have referred to is more fundamental. Its underlying concepts—such as the concept of 'wide-range personal connectivity that you can live in'—seem likely to be with us, in some form, for a while.

Instead of worrying about what might happen to Mark Zuckerberg's company, our time would be better spent figuring out how to translate ideas from the web 2.0 environment to this new environment.

Just as things that work on the Earth may not work on the moon because the gravitational force and the atmosphere are different, products that succeeded in the Google world may not work in the Facebook world. That's because the laws that govern the Google world are largely based on *links*, which reflect interconnections between information, whereas the laws that govern the Facebook world are based on social connections between people. And the new socially networked world is still a very primitive world; soon concepts of trust, authority, social proof and commerce will get operationalized in it. Facebook is not the next Google. It's the template of an emerging new Internet.

Never has there been a more fertile field for viral growth, or for getting large numbers of people habituated to what you can offer them.

29

Inbound Marketing

We have now covered a variety of ways to augment your chances of success—from placing low-cost bets to using the Four Actions Framework, focusing on a specific niche to create traction and cross the chasm, and building in habit formation and virality.

Another valuable continuation to this line of thought is inbound marketing. You have identified your niche by defining your customer avatar. You create useful content for that customer avatar. Such content creates traffic, which leads to conversations. And conversation over time builds enough knowledge to create a community around it.

- ✓ **Create Valuable Content**
- ✓ **Generate Traffic**
- ✓ **Start Conversations**
- ✓ **Increase Valuable Content via Co-Creation with Users**
- ✓ **Have Good Retention of Users**
- ✓ **Build a Community**
- ✓ **Run a Profitable Business**

It's important to start publishing content, generating traffic and building a community as early as possible. Most people wait for their product to be ready before they think of 'creating a buzz.' But you want to get the beehive (i.e., the community) up and running first, for two reasons. You will need the community to help you co-create your product. And, the community becomes your source of revenue!

If you can market to the people who have come streaming in to view your content, that may be the only marketing you will need, and it will certainly be the most cost-effective.

Outbound marketing vehicles like ads and billboards cost a lot of money; they always have waste (i.e. many of the people they reach are not prospective customers), and they are not guaranteed to bring in any revenues. Inbound marketing, on other hand, selects people who are more disposed to buy. You are drawing target customers simply by putting up *content that is relevant to them*, which could be in any number of forms: articles, pictures, videos, audio podcasts, webinars, whitepapers, presentations and forums of all kinds. Also, you do not have to create all of the content yourself from scratch; crowdsourcing can be used to create content.

The best place to start learning about inbound marketing is HubSpot. The founders of that site, Brian Halligan and Dharmesh Shah, coined the terminology and they have posted a great deal of how-to-do-it content. Rather than try to summarize what HubSpot can tell you, I will just recommend that you go there and tell you a story instead.

Inbound Marketing + Z2L Roadmap: Narsi's Story

One of my friends used inbound marketing to get tremendous results for his employer, and then to launch a business of his

own. His name is Narsi Santhanam and his story is a good one for the closing pages of this book, as it also illustrates some key principles of following the Zero to Launch roadmap.

Several years ago Narsi was working at the U.K. office of Sify Technologies, a major India-based Internet company. The main Sify site has a variety of news and ecommerce portals; Narsi was looking at how to build business for the travel-and-tourism pages. After studying how the Google search engine ranks websites, he started creating travel content tailored to his target customers. As the Google rankings went up and traffic increased, he was soon generating more leads than the sales team could handle, along with so much revenue that his organization cut back other marketing efforts and essentially went with his inbound approach.

This initial success was an eye-opener for Narsi. He had found a sweet spot for himself. He enjoyed inbound marketing work, he was pretty good at it, and clearly one could make money from it. Narsi decided to return home to India and begin working on his own.

Over time, he improved and refined his skills. He saw that creating content to generate traffic requires an understanding of the customer, combined with an understanding of how the web works. The first stage is choosing a target segment and learning the persona(s) of the customers and their interests. The next stage entails knowing how to optimize your online presence by techniques like keyword analysis and getting other websites, including high-ranked websites, to link to yours.

Narsi got a firm grasp of all the skills involved. Then he set out to build a website that could grow into a global community around a subject of importance to his home country. And the subject he chose may strike you as extremely odd: castor oil!

Most of us think of castor oil as nothing more than an old-

fashioned folk medicine, which by the way is not pleasant to take. How many people could possibly care to read about the stuff? Narsi, who has an engineering background, knew that the answer was: enough people to make up a very sizable niche market. This oil and its byproducts, made from castor beans, are used worldwide in industries from food processing to biofuels. And the world's leading producer of castor oil happens to be India.

Narsi built the content on his site gradually, guided by feedback and input from visitors. The topics ranged from commercial news and data on the production and uses of castor oil to technical articles on its chemistry. To draw more traffic, Narsi linked to other sites where castor oil was discussed and posted comments. He positioned his own site, www.castoroil.in, as 'The Only Online Bookmark You'll Ever Need for Anything Castor'. It became the single most-visited site on the subject.

Better yet, as his web community grew, Narsi found multiple ways to earn revenue by providing value. He got to know the suppliers of castor oil products, evaluating their strengths and specialties and their ability to export. Soon—in response to a simple invitation on the website—industrial buyers were contacting him to serve as a broker. The income he earned from brokering deals made him financially independent.

He also began producing and updating a 'Comprehensive Castor Oil Report' on the state of the industry. Visitors to the site can download a free overview or buy the full report for several hundred dollars per copy, as firms in industries from pharmaceuticals to electronics have done.

This is the beauty of inbound marketing. Narsi has built a viable global enterprise without, as far as I know, spending a penny to go out and solicit business for his site. Relevant content will drive targeted traffic that can lead to conversations

and community-building. As your community grows, you can sell products and services that benefit the members, which is precisely what Narsi did.

Furthermore, at pivotal times, he applied a number of the start-up principles we have learned about. See how many you can find in his story. Here are several:

- Narsi started with himself as his biggest asset. He found a sweet spot and developed his skills in an area that was new to him, in part while serving an 'apprenticeship' with an existing firm, Sify.
- To start his own business, he interacted with customers early and often. He built out his website at low cost, gradually.
- As the field for the business, he found a blue ocean. The universe of castor oil producers and users is large and far-flung, yet at the time he started, there was no other website recognized as an online hub for the industry.
- Having defined a target market, he focused on that niche. This is what Geoffrey Moore advises in *Crossing the Chasm*, and it's also in keeping with Jim Collins' hedgehog concept. Narsi got really, really good at one thing—serving his niche through a website—to the point where he even became, as Collins suggests, 'the best in the world' at it!

30

Stepping Back
Let's Summarize Our Trip

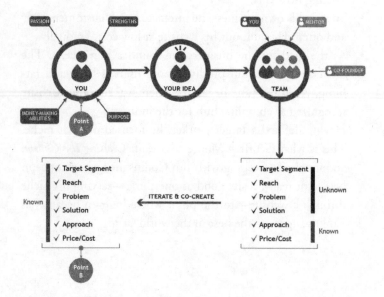

So where are we now? We started with you: your strengths, passions and money-making abilities; your dreams, desires and goals. We saw how a business idea could emerge from knowledge of your assets. Then we covered the processes of adding mentors, and maybe a co-founder, to complete the skill set necessary for start-up.

Next came the steps of figuring out the key parameters for your business—target segment, reach, problem, solution, approach and price/cost. You saw how to convert the unknowns to knowns by co-creating and iteratively testing prototypes of your product, along with customers in your target segment, until you arrive at your MVP, a minimum viable product. Once that occurs, you have moved from point A to point B and your start-up is sustainably *launched*.

If you were only to get two things from this book I would like them to be the following core messages:

1. When you iterate and co-create rapidly, your chances of success increase, sometimes dramatically.
2. By leveraging your strengths, following your passions and aligning with your goals, you will have a much more enjoyable and fulfilling journey. Of course there is much, much more I could tell you. But if you have taken to heart what you've read so far, I think you are ready for the parting words in the pages ahead.

31

Major, Common Mistakes of First-time Entrepreneurs

Given my tendency to focus on positive mental attitude and brightspots, it was not easy for me to include this chapter. However, many people thought a 'roadmap' for entrepreneurs should have a section that explicitly points out the potholes. So here is a list of eleven *major* mistakes to watch out for.

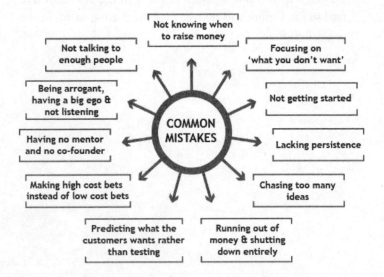

1. **Worrying about what you don't want rather than focusing on what you want.**

    The Law of Attraction says you will attract what you give attention to, regardless of whether you want the object of your attention. This means that you can get what you really, really want. But it also means you will get what you really, really don't want if you give it too much attention! Some entrepreneurs, who are overly focused on the competition, get eaten by the competition. Others, who properly focus on customers and their needs, get a lot of customers and grow quickly to build a profitable business.

2. **Not getting started.**

    Entrepreneurs may procrastinate because they are hanging around negative people who don't think they will succeed; or, they have not broken down the tasks to manageable size, so they perceive getting started as a single, huge, daunting task that stops them dead in their tracks.

3. **Lack of persistence.**

    Giving up too soon is one of the biggest mistakes of first-time entrepreneurs.

4. **Having too many ideas and not testing any idea properly.**

    This is like chasing too many rabbits. You will not catch any of them. I have been guilty of this in the past; it took me a while to realize it and change.

5. **Running out of money before reaching MVP.**

    When this occurs, which it often does, many entrepreneurs seal their fate by committing an additional mistake. They completely shut down their start-ups instead of keeping them alive part-time while working at a job.

6. **Predicting rather than testing.**
   Some entrepreneurs tend to suffer from the delusion that they are mindreaders. They think they know how the customer thinks or, even worse, they believe that they think like the customer! Then they proceed to build a product they want, but nobody else does.

7. **Staking a lot on high-cost bets instead of making frequent low-cost bets.**
   This is one of the surest ways to run out of money before reaching point B.

8. **Not having a coach or a co-founder when you need them.**
   This mistake often stems from being too greedy about equity, unwilling to share. A question to ask yourself is: Would you rather own part of a success or 100% of nothing?

9. **Not listening due to arrogance and ego.**
   If you insist on doing everything 'your way', that isn't a sign of strength; it's a fatal weakness.

10. **Being secretive and not talking to enough people.**
    Perhaps you are afraid that others might steal your ideas. To this I would say: Building an enterprise is a huge endeavour of passion. Other entrepreneurs have their own passions, different from yours. So they are unlikely to steal your ideas, and even if they do, it's unlikely that they will have the passion to make your ideas succeed.

11. **Not knowing how and when to raise money.**
    Some entrepreneurs fail to get the funding their start-ups need, while others raise money too early and for too low a valuation.

We have addressed some of these mistakes—in a more positive manner—previously in the book. The list of *possible* mistakes is surely much longer than eleven. But these are all important ones to avoid, and one 'natural' way to avoid missteps is by having a well-attuned mindset. That is the final subject we will consider.

32

The Mindset of an Entrepreneur

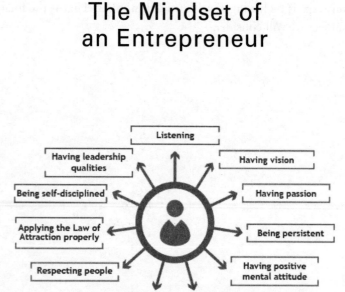

When Robert Kiyosaki talks about changing 'core values' to move from the E (or Employee) quadrant to the B or Business Owner quadrant, he is describing the same process that we call 'creating an entrepreneurial mindset'. For many people, a point of confusion presents itself here. Can such a mindset actually be 'created', or do you just sort of have to be born with it—as I seemed to imply at the beginning of this book, when I said that we entrepreneurs appear to have a 'different DNA' than most people? Maybe the following distinction will help.

The inclination or *desire* to start a business of one's own certainly seems to be inherent in some people much more than in others. This desire, this passion is necessary. Otherwise you won't get far beyond 'Gee, it would be cool to start a business.' But if you have the desire, the traits and habits of mind that enable you to succeed can be learned and cultivated. And since most of these traits and habits are ones that will serve you well in just about any area of life, the only question left is: Why not? Why not start creating the mindset right now?

Many qualities are needed to be an entrepreneur. The graphic shows a number of them. Those I would emphasize include: vision, persistence, great people skills (including the ability to build long-term relationships), patience, persistence, a healthy balance in all aspects of life, applying the law of attraction, *persistence* and the ability to be self-motivated, self-disciplined, and a leader.

If you feel you are missing some of these characteristics, don't worry. Just noticing where you need to improve is an excellent start. (Not to mention an excellent ongoing practice!)

And best of all, while each entrepreneur's journey, including yours, is personal and unique, you will never be alone. Your mentors and other people will be there to support you. You can draw on the insights of those who have travelled similar roads before by reading the books recommended on the next page, and by re-reading this book as needed. You can learn from your customers and from everyone you come in contact with.

Everything you will need, you can find.

Now let the end of this book be your beginning!

Recommended Reading

On the Law of Attraction:
- *The Secret*, by Rhonda Byrne
- *What to Say When You Talk to Yourself*, by Shad Helmstetter
- *The Parable of the Homemade Millionaire*, by Bryan James

On People Skills:
- *How to Win Friends and Influence People*, by Dale Carnegie

On Relationships:
- *Bringing Out the Best in People*, by Alan Loy McGinnis
- *The 5 Love Languages*, by Gary Chapman

On Business:
- *Rich Dad, Poor Dad* and *The Business School*, by Robert Kiyosaki
- *The Innovator's Dilemma* and other books by Clayton Christensen
- *Blue Ocean Strategy*, by W. Chan Kim and Renee Mauborgne
- *Crossing the Chasm*, by Geoffrey A. Moore
- *The Four Steps to the Epiphany*, by Steven Gary Blank

On Sales/Approach:
- *How I Raised Myself from Failure to Success in Selling*, by Frank Bettger
- *Inbound Marketing*, by Brian Halligan and Dharmesh Shah

Some Great Books in General:

- *The Black Swan* and *Fooled by Randomness,* by Nassim Nicholas Taleb
- *Switch,* by Chip Heath and Dan Heath
- *Influencer,* by Kerry Patterson, Joseph Grenny, David Maxfield and Ron McMillan
- *The Passion Test*, by Janet Bray Attwood and Chris Attwood

Acknowledgements

I take this opportunity to thank many people. When you write a book that is a result of your experience and your experience spans a couple of decades, there are countless people to thank! They include hundreds of authors of books. They include many people I have worked with, clients that have contributed to my learning, the many co-founders that I have had the good fortune of associating with, the many start-ups that I have either invested in or mentored over the years, and of course friends, family and others who were in one way or the other involved in my education process. There is no way I can name all of them or hope to remember all the people who have helped me in my journey so far. But I know from my heart that I am grateful; grateful to live in these wonderful times and be touched by all these magical people. It's with gratitude and joy that I share this book with all of you. I really, really hope, wish and pray that it will save countless hours of misery and frustration for countless numbers of new entrepreneurs.

The key authors who have shaped my thinking (and their books that benefited me the most) include: Clayton Christensen (*Innovator's Solution* in particular), W. Chan Kim and Renee Mauborgne (*Blue Ocean Strategy*), Geoffrey Moore (*Crossing the Chasm*), Nassim Taleb (*The Black Swan*), Robert Kiyosaki (*Rich Dad, Poor Dad*), Rhonda Byrne (*The Secret*), Esther and

Jerry Hicks (*The Law of Attraction*), Bryan James (*The Parable of the Homemade Millionaire*), Dan Ariely (*Predictably Irrational*), Brad Feld and David Cohen (*Do More Faster: TechStars Lessons to Accelerate Your Startup*), Jason Fried and David Heinemeier Hansson (*Rework*), Kerry Patterson, Joseph Grenny, David Maxfield, Ron McMillan and Al Switzler (*Influencer: The Power to Change Anything*), Chip Heath and Dan Heath (*Switch: How to Change Things When Change Is Hard*), Chris Anderson (*The Long Tail: Why the Future of Business Is Selling Less of More*), Dan Senor and Saul Singer (*Start-up Nation: The Story of Israel's Economic Miracle*), Steven D. Levitt and Stephen J. Dubner (*Freakonomics: A Rogue Economist Explores the Hidden Side of Everything*), Richard H. Thaler and Cass R. Sunstein (*Nudge*), Atul Gawande (*The Checklist Manifesto*), James Surowiecki (*The Wisdom of Crowds*), Gary Vaynerchuk (*Crush It! Why NOW Is the Time to Cash In on Your* Passion), Timothy Ferriss (*The 4-Hour Workweek: Escape 9-5, Live Anywhere, and Join the New Rich*), Malcolm Gladwell (*Outliers: The Story of Success*), Jim Collins (*Good to Great: Why Some Companies Make the Leap and Others Don't*), Guy Kawasaki (*The Art of the Start*), Daniel Pink (*Drive*), Michael E. Gerber (*The E-Myth Revisited: Why Most Small Businesses Don't Work and What to Do about It*), Porus Munshi (*Making Breakthrough Innovation Happen: How 11 Indians Pulled Off the Impossible*).

Also, I thank teachers and authors on other important topics, including Steven Blank, Eric Ries (*The Lean Startup*), Ash Maurya (*Running Lean*), Dave McClure, Hiten Shah, Alexander Osterwalder and Professor Yves Pigneur (*The Business Model Generation*), Brian Halligan and Dharmesh Shah (*Inbound Marketing*), Seth Godin, Robert Scoble, Steve Garfield, Clay Collins, George Kao, Jack Canfield and Mark Victor Hansen (*Chicken Soup for the Soul* series), Sramana Mitra (1Mx1M initiative).

Some key people who have helped me immensely in my learnings over the years include my wife, Shaku Miriyala, my parents Sunanda and Murthy Miriyala, my children Avani Miriyala and Akash Miriyala, my sister, Dr Lakshmi Yamujala, G. Venkat, Chinna Boddipalli, Dr Sudesh Kannan, Prasad Rao, Seshadri Guha, Kulin Desai, Srinivas Vemu, Swadeep Pillarisetti, Narsimhan Santhanam, Narayan Reddy, Srinivas Makam, Dorian Duka, Joe Abraham, Raju Anthony, Tiger Ramesh, Amit Sethi, Phaneesh Murthy, Mathew Cyriac, Ramu Sunkara, Vijay Tella, Bhaskar Roy, Nikolay Abkairov, James Dias, Krishna Pendyala, Sukhwant Khanuja, Aravind Reddy, Dheeraj Reddy, Raghunath Sapuram, Mohammed Farooq, Nandan Lexman, Dr Nirup Krishnamurthy, Vishal Srivastava, Sanchita Sur, Guru Bhoopala, Sanjay Kadaveru and Bhaskar Enaganti.

I thank Reethika Sunder for her persistence, diligence and absolute belief that this stuff should come out of my head and be in print for others to read. I cannot really thank her enough for the endless hours of work, sacrifice and sleepless nights. But for her, this would not have happened.

—Kanth Miriyala

It's great to be associated with this book not only because of the tremendous learning during its creation but also the sheer pleasure of working with Kanth. He has been my mentor and guide and I am glad I could help him share his knowledge and experience in the form of a book for first-time entrepreneurs. For helping me through my journey in life, I would like to thank my parents, Shashikala and M. R. Sunder, and all my friends.

If I start to mention the list of authors I have grown up reading and that inspired me to write a book and create something beautiful of my own someday, I would easily fill many pages of this book. Probably the first step was to help make this a reality

for Kanth. My best friends through childhood and probably for the rest of my life will be books and I hope this book also creates the fascination and awe that every book I have read in life has done for me. I can never thank authors enough for the meaning they add to life.

I would also like to thank Mike Vargo for helping us make this book an easy read and Adrian Dragne for helping us with the graphics.

—Reethika Sunder

About the Authors

Hello! I am KANTH MIRIYALA. Nice meeting you!

I had my first brush with entrepreneurship quite by accident. I think everyone should own their own business; nothing would please me more than to start a school of entrepreneurship. But that's later. For now, I am settling for a book on the subject!

I was one of the co-founders for Quintant, which got sold to iGATE in 2003. I thought I would retire in 2007, but it got boring real soon. So I decided I would 'stay in touch' with high tech and became an early stage investor in Qik, a mobile video streaming company, later sold to Skype for over $100 million; in turn Skype got sold a couple of months later to Microsoft. Between Qik, a few start-ups that did not make it and a few other start-ups that are in the pipeline, I managed to 'practise' my methodology for start-ups.

I did my engineering from IIT Madras and have a PhD, but that's only because I did not know when to stop studying!

If you like our book, please join us on Facebook and Twitter and visit our website www.e5to9.com. And let all your friends know about the book! We also request you to support the book by writing a review on your blog or website or by sending a testimonial to entrepreneur5to9@gmail.com.

Hello! I am REETHIKA SUNDER.

I hope you enjoyed reading this book and learnt as much as I did while I was helping Kanth write it. It changed my perspective about start-ups requiring you to either quit your job or involving huge investments. This book allays the fears that keep you from dreaming and doing what you really want to.

I love wildlife and spend most of my vacations visiting forests. I love travelling and also like painting, which is a newfound love. My interests keep changing and I have tried various things, from kickboxing to theatre to salsa. Like everything else in life, some interests stay and some wane away with time. Writing is something that has stayed.

I did my MBA in Marketing from IIM Ahmedabad and now work as a consultant with an Indian IT firm.